No Strangers in Exile

No Strangers in Exile

A Novel by Hans Harder

Freely Translated from the German,
Edited, and Expanded
by Al Reimer

HYPERION PRESS LIMITED   Winnipeg, Manitoba, Canada
for the Mennonite Literary Society and the University of Winnipeg

Published for the Mennonite Literary Society and the University of Winnipeg
Published in the United States by Herald Press, Scottdale, Pa. 15683

International Standard Book Number: 0-8361-1898-7
Canadian SBN: 0-920534-07-4

Printed and bound by Derksen Printers, Steinbach, Manitoba, Canada
Designed and illustrated by Arlene Osen

10 9 8 7 6 5 4 3 2 1

In memory of the thousands of Mennonite exiles in Russia, strangers in their own land, known and unknown, alive or dead, of whatever time or place, who shared their cruel and senseless fate with millions of their countrymen.

The Mennonite Literary Society, Inc., and the Chair in Mennonite Studies of the University of Winnipeg are pleased to make available this second volume in a series of English translations dealing with the Mennonite experience in the Soviet Union. Once again, Al Reimer has undertaken the job of translating and editing the original manuscript. We are grateful to him for his creative and faithful rendering of the spirit and intent of the original novel by Hans Harder. We would like to thank the Multicultural Program, Government of Canada, for the grant which assisted in the publication of this volume. Special thanks must be given to Marvis Tutiah, editor and publisher of Hyperion Press, and to her partner, Arlene Osen, who designed the book and provided the illustrations.

We trust that this second volume, like the first, *A Russian Dance of Death,* will prove to be of interest not only to mature readers but also to younger readers who are not acquainted with the events described. Hans Harder's novel is a moving portrayal of the hardships experienced by many people in the Soviet Union in the 1930s. It describes experiences that, terrible as they were, must be kept alive in the consciousness of the present generation, and we can be thankful to writers like Hans Harder and Al Reimer for their sensitive recreation of those bitter events and times.

Roy Vogt
President
Mennonite Literary Society, Inc.

Harry Loewen
Chair in Mennonite Studies
University of Winnipeg

Contents

The Author   *ix*

Introduction   *1*

Prologue   *5*

Part I   The Wind Blows North   *7*

Part II   Our Bitter Bread   *31*

Part III   Escape The Wild Wind   *71*

Part IV   More Than Bread   *103*

Epilogue   *125*

Hans Harder was born in 1903 in Neuhoffnung, one of the eight villages of the Mennonite settlement of Alexandertal in the province of Samara (now Kuybychev) not far from Uljanovsk on the Volga. After the Russian Revolution, his father, a businessman, decided to move his family back to its ancestral home in West Prussia. Young Harder attended the University of Königsberg, and for a time was active in Arnold's *Bruderhof* movement in various parts of Germany.

From 1928-33 Harder was busy as editor and publisher (the Hans Harder Verlag). A man of strong principles and fearless integrity, he did not hesitate to take an anti-Nazi stand when Hitler rose to power. He withdrew from the Hamburg Mennonite Church because it contained many avowed Nazis. From 1933 until the end of World War II he was active in the Confessing Church. In 1946 he was appointed Professor of Sociology at the Pedagogical Academy in Wuppertal and remained there until his retirement in 1968. He then began a new career as minister and elder of the Frankfurt Mennonite Church. He now enjoys an active retirement in Schlüchtern.

Harder's first novel, *In Wologdas weissen Wälder* (1934) was followed by a remarkable spate of seven novels published between 1937 and 1942. Although written for readers in Germany, all of these novels are set in Russia and most of them deal with the experience of Mennonite colonists slightly disguised as German colonists. The three novels that are most specifically Mennonite in setting and treatment are *Das Dorf an der Wolga (The Village on the Volga)* 1937, *Das sibirische Tor (The Siberian Gate)* 1938, and *Die Hungerbrüder (Brothers in Hunger)* 1938. Harder chose not to resume his career as a novelist after the War, but he has continued to write and publish on a wide range of subjects. For years he cherished a plan to write a cycle of novels that would span the entire history of the Mennonites, but the plan did not come to fruition.

What Hans Harder has achieved, however, places him in the front rank among Mennonite writers, although his own assessment of his writing is characteristically frank and modest: "I have never lost the feeling that in my achievements I have fallen far short of my goal. Whatever I have achieved makes me bow humbly before Him who made me write about my brethern (in Russia) whose fate and labors I want to save from oblivion in a confused world." In the words of Cornelius Krahn, Mennonite historian and critic, "Hans Harder is unquestionably one of the best writers using Mennonite themes that Mennonitism has produced." It is a judgment that Harder's many readers would heartily endorse.

Introduction

In recent years many writers—foremost among them Aleksandr Solzhenitsyn—have begun to document the tragic story of the Stalinist forced labor
camps. Few if any such writings existed in 1934 when Hans Harder, using the
pseudonym Alexander Schwarz, published this novel in Germany as *In
Wologdas weissen Waelder*. It preceded even such an early prison classic as
Arthur Koestler's *Darkness at Noon*.

As a German Mennonite survivor of the Russian Revolution, Hans Harder
knew at first hand what was happening in his native land. He wished to alert
the Western world to the systematic brutality and oppression being practised
on a massive scale in the Soviet Union. In his Preface the author declared
frankly that his motive for writing the novel was more political than literary.
He said he wanted "to sound warning bells to the world [that] in Russia whole
groups of people are dying, among them one and a half million surviving German [colonists]. The alarm is sounded for their sake . . .. Our brothers in
Russia do not want sympathy, only fair treatment."

The turbulence and chaos of the Revolution and Civil War were followed by
the relatively calm and stable period of the New Economic Policy (1921-29),
during which Soviet citizens were again able to lead more or less regular
lives. In the Kremlin, however, a wily Georgian was quietly consolidating his
power. By 1929 Stalin was ready to make his move. His plan was to break the
stubborn resistance of Russia's rural masses by forcing them onto collective
farms *(kolkhozy)*. As part of this policy, there was a ruthless drive to
eliminate all *kulaks*, vaguely defined as farmers who owned, or had owned,
their own land, equipment, and stock. A man's possession of a cow or two was
often enough for him to be relegated to this category. Thus began an un-
precedented period of mass persecution and organized violence by the state.
Millions of people were forcibly uprooted and arbitrarily sentenced to lengthy
terms at hard labor in the work camps that were springing up all over the
vast land.

As Solzhenitsyn has recently shown, the Communist forced labor camps of the Gulag had their origins not in Siberia, as had been generally supposed, but in the far north, specifically in the notorious Solovki Islands in the White Sea off Archangel. From there they spread like a slow cancer through the length and breadth of the Soviet Union in the thirties and forties.

The early camps in the north were mainly logging camps set up in wilderness places without names under the most appallingly primitive conditions. The workers required for these camps were plucked almost at random from various parts of the country. The timber that was cut in vast quantities at the cost of countless lives was exported mainly to western Europe, much of it to Germany. Solzhenitsyn gives a grim description of the northern camps:

> . . . We are not able to enumerate the countless logging camps. They constitute half the Archipelago . . .. On what maps or in whose memory have all these thousands of temporory logging camps been preserved, camps established for one year, for two, for three, until all the woods nearby had been cut, and then removed lock, stock and barrel? [1]

One of these logging camps, the focus of this story, is Camp Number 513 (fictitious in this case) on the Mezen River. Its exact location cannot be determined from the text, but it lay not far due east of Archangel and the Solovki Islands.

While *No Strangers in Exile* is a work of fiction, it is closely based on fact. The main group of characters consists of simple, devout German Mennonite colonists from the village of Mariental in the Alexandertal settlement in Samara Province (slightly disguised in the novel as Saratov Province, which lies along the Volga just to the south of Samara). Alexandertal consisted of ten villages with a combined population of well over a thousand. Founded in 1861, it was the last of the four original Mennonite settlements founded in Russia after 1789. By World War I there were another forty daughter settlements dotting the Russian plains from the Ukraine to Siberia. By that time the total Mennonite population in Russia had risen to about one hundred thousand. These German-speaking Mennonites were highly successful farmers; they were also breaking into the world of business and the professions when they were stopped short by the Revolution.

Hans Harder himself is a native of Alexandertal and knows his characters thoroughly, although he was no longer living in Russia during the period covered by the novel. Like millions of their countrymen these Mennonite settlers from the Volga fell victim to Stalin's savage campaign of dekulakization. Their "crime" was that they had once been successful farmers. And at this early stage of the camp system it was not only the men who were sent into exile as "voluntary resettlers", but their wives and children as well. The courage and staunch faith shown by these decent, peaceful Mennonites as they try to make the best of their bleak circumstances illuminate the pages of Harder's novel from first to last.

This English version is not a straightforward translation of the German text. Rather, it is what the translator regards as a "creative" translation, that is, a free translation which contains some minor changes in plot, characteriza-

---

[1] Aleksandr I. Solzhenitsyn, *The Gulag Archipelago Two* (New York, 1975), p. 593.

tion, and point of view, as well as numerous changes of a stylistic nature. When I undertook to translate this novel, I realized that some changes would be necessary in order to give it the right appeal for a new generation of English readers far removed in time and place from the historical period and the cultural traditions in which the book was rooted. My major concerns were to soften the rather overt didacticism of the novel without weakening its Christian theme and to de-emphasize its rather obvious strategy to enlist the sympathies of readers in Germany during the thirties.

In rewriting I have tried to respect the author's intentions and, in places, to realize those intentions more fully. Thus, I have added some new material and deleted some passages of the original text. The result is an English version which, while not a complete rewriting of the original, is considerably more than a simple translation. What I have striven for are greater dramatic impact and readability.

I wish to add that I had the author's generously granted written permission to make whatever alterations to the text I deemed necessary. It is my sincere hope that I have not abused his trust and that this reconstituted version of the novel will meet with the approval of English readers. A story of such tragic import as this one is should not be allowed to die.

Al Reimer
February 1979

Prologue

In centuries preceding our own, writers often wrote works of fiction in order to add complexity to the reality in which they lived. In our century many a writer finds it necessary to reverse that process and create works of fiction to simplify the incredible complexity of the world in which we live. *No Strangers in Exile* belongs to the latter category of twentieth century works of fiction. The events characterized here take place in Soviet Russia during the 1930s, a period when Joseph Stalin or The Man of Steel was entangling one-sixth of the world with barbed wire.

The narrative is focused on the so-called Volga-Germans, those German Mennonite farmers who settled in Russia during the reign of Alexander II in the nineteenth century. Now, in the 1930s, whole families and whole villages of these hard-working farmers were transformed into "voluntary resettlers" by the Soviet government and were exiled to the northern extremities of that vast empire. The camp described in this work is located somewhere between the city of Archangelsk and the northern end of the Ural Mountains.

The prisoners work in the forest, cutting trees, which the Soviet government exports to West European countries. They suffer from hunger, cold, typhus, and from psychological depression induced by the hopeless situation of their ambiguous existence. Among them are righteous and gentle people, such as Ohm Peters and orthodox priest, Father Nikolai. There are restless and defiant people in their midst, and others, such as young Theresa, willing to sell themselves to the camp authorities.

The prisoners work, pray, write letters to their relatives in Germany—but "voluntary resettlers" they remain. Some manage to escape from the camp, and one even succeeds in reaching Leningrad. There, in Leningrad, no one dares to assist the escapee. What is more, the "free citizens" also live under conditions resembling those in which the "voluntary resettlers" exist. There is scarcity of food in Leningrad; police spies are surveying the population; and there is an all-pervading fear affecting the residents. The escapee finds neither safety nor freedom there, and it is with a degree of relief that he capitulates when he is captured and sent back to the prison camp.

The novel begins nowhere, so to speak, and it ends nowhere—a literary device fully consonant with the essential character of the subject matter.

The effect of this work on the reader is one of ambiguity, puzzlement, and bewilderment . . .

Why do we allow ourselves to be herded and molested?

Who authorizes anyone to treat human beings in this way?

How does a system with such complex entrapments arise?

Who creates it and why?

What are we, these creatures who brutalize our fellow-humans without apparent felling of remorse?

There are no answers to such distrubing questions in this work, but a sensitive reader is compelled to ask these and many other such questions.

Paul Call
Professor of Russian History
The University of Manitoba

Part I
The Wind Blows North

The wind blows south, the wind blows north,
round and round it goes full circle. Ecclesiastes 1:6

"—three hundred ninety-seven, three hundred ninety-eight, three hundred ninety-nine. Get the hell moving into those cars!"

Dark forms huddling awkwardly around the doors pant and groan as they jump, climb, and push each other into the boxcars. A noisy crescendo of rattling boxes and thumping sacks. Then the sliding doors clank shut.

"Goodbye, Little Mother Moscow," somebody shouts outside.

Freight train Number 6259 starts out laboriously along the solitary line that runs from Moscow through Yaroslavl and Vologda to the Far North. We are sitting in ancient, crudely renovated cattle cars on whose exterior walls a bold hand has clumsily chalked the words *"dobrovol'nye pereselentsy"* (voluntary resettlers). The broad sliding doors on both sides keep shifting in their grooves, but remain securely locked. What little we are able to glimpse of the world rushing by we see through an opening under the slightly arched ceiling. As a peephole the opening is big enough, but as a window it lacks a pane. It is essential for our transport, however: through this opening, presumably, they will serve us early each morning and at noon our pailful of hot millet gruel or something similar.

It is the eighteenth of October, 1930. The thermometer, which I was able to shove into my pocket when I was arrested, drops hourly until by early evening it reaches minus sixteen degrees centigrade.

Yes, Alexander Harms, I reflect ruefully, for you and for these others the temperature will probably continue to drop until the mercury hits bottom. I am sitting in the rear car, surrounded by German-Mennonite farm families

Route of exile to the camps in Russia's far north.

from our colony in Saratov Province on the Volga. Across from me sits my old friend and neighbor, Peter Koehn, from our village of Mariental. For six years we shared a bench in the village school and remained close friends in later years when he was a farmer and I a teacher. As I gaze at Koehn's short, stocky figure and at his broad, open face, cheerful even in this alien setting, I recall again what we have lost. Our idyllic old colony with its farms of up to two thousand acres and each farm's three dozen horses — all that was swept away long ago. We'll never see any of it again. Bit by bit, through twelve years of "requisitioning", harrassment, and frequent arrests we became conditioned to the harsh new world of the collective. But even that was not the end of our downfall. The brutal labor on the collective was only a prologue to the sudden mass arrests and exile.

Yes, Peter, I address him silently, you and I have no illusions left. At least you still have Maria and your four kids with you. Not like some others in our transport . . . . Well, it's all over now, and you musn't blame yourself for what happened. It wasn't your fault that your sick horse dropped dead in the midst of the fall work on the collective. That pathetic accident was only a convenient excuse to brand us all as *"kulak* saboteurs." Sooner or later the local soviet would have found some other pretext. Nobody's blaming you. You are as innocent as the rest of us.

As I gaze at the familiar faces near me my thoughts race on and I continue my private assessments. Next to Koehn sits Hans Neufeld, our tough, shrewd village official and district mayor in the old days. I never liked you much even then, I admit to myself. Oh yes, you conducted our village affairs with an iron hand. Nobody ever got the better of you, did they? Where's your authority now, Hans? Like the rest of us you've been forced to play a new role. You're a bitter, broken old man and I pity you. But I know you have learned nothing. Like a child petulant after losing, you sulk and whine and demand that the game be played over again. But it won't be, my friend. Ever. Your reign is over. All you have left is your sour old wife. Even your children deserted you long ago.

And there, nodding by the wall, is William Penner, our taciturn village carpenter, with eyes like stones and face, as always, inscrutable behind the shaggy black beard. You were the homespun philosopher of our community, my friend, with your quaint little rustic library and your Fritz Reuter[1] evenings. Now you're more withdrawn than ever. And with good reason. You've had some tough knocks, losing your children one by one and your one surviving child retarded. The boy sits beside you now sharing the senseless fate that struck us all that night five weeks ago. And we understand these events no better than your child does.

And you Diedka Tielmann, my former colleague! How well I remember when you came to our school fresh from the Teaching Institute in Moscow. You were a dashing young idealist, dark and smiling, eager to burnish the minds of our raw farm boys with the culture you had acquired. When the bad

---

[1]Fritz Reuter was a nineteenth-century German writer whose shrewd, humorous peasant stories in Low German were immensely popular with Russian Mennonites.

times came, you dared to stand on principle. To save your conscience, you swapped your lectern for a plough as early as '24. "Better no school at all," you said, "than an atheistic one." Fearlessly, you showed us that it is possible to take a moral stand even in a communist state. You will always be remembered for that.

I break off my silent monologue as my mind is jolted back to a more recent event. One man is missing from our group. He is Peter Albrecht, another farmer from our village. Across from me in the corner his wife and five-year-old boy have been weeping for him since we left Moscow. Just before our departure two policemen came and took him away on some thread of suspicion. He must have been sent to his final destiny by a shorter route than ours.

With Mrs. Albrecht is her elderly father, Ohm[2] Jasch Peters, who belongs not only to her but to all of us. Ohm Jasch is a devout, unpretentious old man whose strong, simple faith is our pillar of fire in this dark night. He is our minister. The oldest among us, he has been our unfailing counselor and consoler during the desolate weeks that our little group has been traveling across Russia. More than anyone, he is our link with the world we once lived in, believed in, felt comfortable in. Thanks to his presence, we are still a civilized little community: a human family in spite of this unspeakable degradation.

The remainder of the exiles in our transport come from different regions: from the Caucasus, the Volga, the Ukraine, and even Siberia. They are drawn from various racial groups but they share a common identity now which transcends ethnic and cultural identities. In exile there are no strangers—only brothers, known or not yet known.

The women are sitting on rough wooden bunks, the men on boxes and chests. The older children, muffled in old shawls, sit or squat among the bundles, boxes, and suitcases. The women have wound dingy blankets around themselves and are listlessly holding the smallest children on their laps. The men sit slumped with eyes shut and heads drooping over calloused hands. Lines of bitterness are etched into their grimy faces. The mechanical rhythm of the train wheels seems to transform us all into swaying puppets bereft of will and consciousness.

The monotonous, unmarked hours continue to crawl by.

When my depressing thoughts come back again full circle, I seek to escape them by clambering over the litter on the floor and stationing myself at the peephole, holding my fur sleeves across my face as protection from the cold. By looking at something out there—anything—one can at least forget one's miseries for a few moments. But the view outside is also depressing: only isolated, squalid little villages occasionally glide into sight along the tracks. All around them yawns the empty steppe—endless, grey Russia!

Our train passes slowly through a district station where hordes of starving, homeless children are milling about begging for food, even from each other. All around the station derelict peasants camp out in the open. Like the children, they also have the desperate look of the starving. Just beyond Alex-

---

[2]This is a title of respect conferred on ministers and other prominent senior members in Russian-Mennonite communities.

androv, I spot the first corpses sprawled beside the tracks; the sight of these emaciated bodies is not exactly consoling. But soon the empty spaces again surround us, and our moving prison becomes ever more unbearable. Now utterly desolate, I return to my seat.

One day, two, three . . .. Time has lost its meaning for our stupified human cargo.

We have left Yaroslavl behind. Outside, on both sides, towers the dark forest. Thick underbrush obscures the birch and alder trunks up to their branches. The trees glide by like a smooth black wall.

Ohm Peters is sitting on his massive trunk with his back against the cold door-wall, which is studded all over with hard beads of frost. He has pulled the broad collar of his sheepskin all the way up and is observing the tree tops sweeping by. He is probably thinking how ominous they look falling away in the night as though struck down in a violent rush.

"Today is the fourth day," Tielmann says suddenly from the other side. He tries to make his voice heard over the clatter of the boxcar wheels as he pulls a long, rusty nail out of his coat pocket and scratches another mark on the wall behind him.

The old man looks at him with a smile and says: "There is Someone marking time for us all, no matter how endless it gets as we move farther north." He leans forward and, putting a horny hand to his mouth, adds: "Tielmann, there is no time here; it has lost itself in space." He points to the window.

"Not to be able to count anymore—that's horrible Ohm Jasch!" the teacher shouts back over the sleeping forms between them.

After a long time the train brakes to a stop again. One of Koehn's boys bumps full force against the bunk. He is more frightened than hurt, as the pillow formed by several coats and blankets affords protection even against the braking of a Russian freight train. His single outcry is all we hear.

Outside somebody is climbing up the side of the car. At the window a fist appears and a voice that has become familiar croaks: "Look alive there—the pail!"

Several pairs of hands reach up for it. Steam rises from the large, misshapen leaden vessel.

"They're coming again—" howls Ohm Peters' little grandson in his sleep and breaks into a crying fit.

"Shhh," the grandfather runs his hand soothingly over the blond head of the troubled child. He lifts him onto his lap. The boy looks around the circle of faces. "Where is—?"

"It's all right," the old man interrupts tenderly. "He'll be coming soon."

We dig our spoons out of pockets and bags. Some self-consciously hold their chilled hands over the hot vapor until the moisture drips from their soiled hands. The boy's outburst has made us hesitate to begin the meal, as our Mariental group is reminded again if the ugly scene in Moscow when the police came for Albrecht just as we were to start eating in the compound behind the station before boarding the train. When they saw us bowing for grace they swore loudly, kicked several of us, and spat into our pot of soup. Now Ohm Peters removes his cap and closes his eyes. We bow our heads silently for a few moments, then timorously guide hot spoonfuls of soup to cold lips while the train sluggishly begins to move again.

Another evening. At the window the silhouettes of trees dissolve into a blackened mass. Night and its solitude are about to overwhelm us again. Another twelve hours of unrelieved isolation ahead. Everyone will either sleep fitfully or continue to stare at the murky walls.

Suddenly the brakes screech. Car wheels grating on steel produce a nerve-rending sound. The train comes to a shuddering stop.

"Tcherti kulaki" (kulak devils), the transport leader curses loudly outside. "What has happened?" we ask each other. Up ahead a boxcar door crashes open, then a second, and a third—the sounds are getting closer. Now our door is being unlocked.

"Out, you bourgeois—damn pigs," the transport leader mangles his words angrily. He stands there squat and red-faced, his tall cossack fur cap conspicuous, its red crown faded to a pale rose.

We jump down quickly and extend a hand to the women and children. It's good to feel ground under our feet again! We drink in the cold, fresh night air eagerly; the change from the stagnant air of the car is so sudden we feel giddy.

We have stopped near a small country station. There must be a village close by, but it is not visible from where we are standing. Something glimmering in the snow beside the rail embankment a few meters away catches my eye. I walk over and find the huddled body of a woman covered by a thin film of ice. I break the crust and feel her arm. She is frozen stiff.

"Fall in!" bawls Fur Cap. Four hundred people in fur coats and shawls that trail behind on the slippery ground sway forward. One old woman, a child in her arms, slips and falls heavily. The ice-crust shatters under her like brittle glass. Somebody gives her a hand and, groaning, she heaves herself to her feet, the baby still clutched to her ample bosom.

"Stoi!" roars the Red. I glance up and down the ranks. In our wild assortment of fur coats, mantles, blankets, shawls, and felt boots we are a motley-looking crew, and no mistake! We resemble Napoleon's army on the retreat from Moscow—except that we're going north.

"We're standing here like the trees behind us—ready to fall," Tielmann whispers beside me.

Pushing back his fur cap with well-lined gloves, the transport leader, priming himself with fierce obscenities, loudly explains that he has examined his list thoroughly and found one prisoner missing.

"Sudermann, Henry! Where is he?"

We look at each other blankly. Nobody can recall seeing that pale student Sudermann since Moscow. He may have escaped, but if he did none of us knew about it. No one can answer Fur Cap's question, although many of us know who he is.

The forest behind us stands immobile and silent. The guards' bayonets gleam weakly in the semi-darkness. From time to time there is a stuttering cough from the locomotive. Still nobody answers.

"Answer me!" screams Fur Cap as he swivels his eyes across the lines of shivering people. He strides up and down nervously. Now he stops before old Peters.

"Citizen Train Leader—it's, it's true that we saw the student in Moscow, but no one seems to know what happened to him—." Peters wants to add something but a curse cuts him off.

"I'll give you—! Maybe some of you still confuse this trip with an excursion to the seaside, you *kulak* sons-of-bitches!" Beside himself with rage, the transport leader yanks off his cap and waves it under Peters' nose. "You'll be cured. Petya, half rations starting tomorrow!"

We are underway again. The train's dreary chant continues unbroken. Clack—clack-clack—clack—clack-clack. It's getting harder to breathe. Somebody has covered up the peephole. I listen enviously to the snoring. If only the cold would stop seeping through my limbs, how gratefully I'd fall asleep too. But I'm not the only one who hasn't been able to sleep during the past four days. I get up stiffly and force myself through a set of brisk calesthenics for a quarter of an hour, then repeat them. Feeling a little warmer, I sit down and try to relax . . . .

If only morning would reveal all this as just a bad dream! To find oneself free again—no matter where or under what circumstances. To be out of this stifling boxcar, to command one's own movements, to eat one's fill once more—these are the simple luxuries for which we would give everything except life itself. In the past six weeks I have mulled over in my mind endlessly all the things that have happened to me in my thirty-five years. My brain is a swirling vortex that keeps sucking me down into the past. There is one part of my life that is especially painful to think about; yet it keeps forcing its way into my memory . . . .

I must try to focus my thoughts on something positive. With proper concentration, for example, I could mentally write a kind of cultural history of our Mennonite colonies here in the midst of Russian society. There have been five generations of successful colonization on the Russian steppes. I could describe in minute detail the prosperous colonies with their large, solid farm houses, abundant gardens, well-tilled fields and splendid stock, and energetic and devout farm families with their devotion to tradition and their German language and customs. "Russia," I could write, "you have been a loving mother to your German sons too." I wouldn't leave that out. What a fine story it would make if I could end it there. But of course I couldn't. To be complete my history would also have to include what has happened to our people since the Glorious October Revolution. When I remember this my heart quails and I am sunk in deep dejection again.

And then the memory of my present tragedy overwhelms me.

"Oh Liese, Liese," my heart cries, "it was such a short time we had together . . . eleven months and nine days exactly."

How I wish I could forget! My survival is at stake. I can no longer afford to remember that night. To an exile hatred and grief are more dangerous than hunger and cold. But the years cannot close the deep wound that keeps dripping red into my consciousness.

It's almost twelve years since they killed you . . . those drunken Cossacks running from the Reds. A thousand times I've asked myself why they chose our little cottage in the schoolyard when there were large, inviting farms all around. Were they sent by Satan to destroy our innocent happiness? . . . Our first year of marriage, you plump and rosy in your seventh month . . . . They forced me to watch . . . on our marriage bed . . . the delicate eggshell of your belly crushed under the iron knees and rutting thighs of those besotted brutes. One after the other they vomited their filth . . . until I felt my soul exploding in a black froth of rage and horror . . . .

And then your screams in the hospital . . . the baby stillborn. It was more than I could bear . . . . When I looked at you small and spent in your coffin, I could not even weep—or pray. I could only stare dully and curse them, and myself. I felt that I was somehow to blame, that it was I who had made your fatal desecration by those monsters possible. In my mad grief I swore never to go near another woman again . . . . Yes, I was mad then, but even later, when the madness was gone, I knew I could never love any other woman as I had loved you . . . .

But enough. Memories of private grief will not warm the thin blood of a starving exile.

We reach Vologda on the fifth day. The dismal-looking station dampens whatever expectations have been aroused by the long journey. Even so, we take inquisitive turns at the peephole. Every free person we see in the station is an object of curiosity. I see a scruffy-looking railway official, a swarm of *bezprizorniki*[3] dressed in loathsome rags. They are all free! How I yearn to join them, to saunter around like that of my own volition.

I try to get the attention of Fur Cap, who is rushing by.

"Hey—Citizen Transport Leader—would you be so kind, the honey pail—?" He doesn't see or hear me.

A *bezprizornik* slinks over to our car. "Comrade," croaks the tiny creature, looking up with his old-wrinkled face, "a piece of bread?"

His gnome's grin reveals an almost toothless mouth. One side of his face is covered with a festering rash. I have seen them in Saratov, in Moscow— everywhere. This one seems to be the end-product of these degenerate times.

"Little Uncle," he wheedles, and from his loose, ragged sleeve glides a filthy hand. It too is covered with sores and looks repulsive. I grope in my pocket for

[3]The word means "homeless children" and refers to orphans who had been made homeless as the result of war and revolution. For many years they plagued Russian cities like packs of marauding jackals, begging, stealing, and looting.

a piece of rusk and throw it to him. The crust misses him, bounces on the frozen ground and is immediately snapped up by one of the other urchins.

"Burzhui prokhatyn, you damn bourgeois!"

His face contorted with sudden rage, the boy leaps up against the side of the boxcar with frightening agility, claws at the door, and in a split second is halfway up. With a sudden jolt the train begins to move and the boy falls. He utters a shrill scream as his body thuds down beside the track. I watch in horror as the wheels slice off his legs.

Our train rolls slowly out of Vologda and stops on a gentle rise. The town lies to our left. In spite of its having been an ancient seat of government, Vologda is quite small, an unimpressive-looking provincial city. Its lacklustre greyness is touched up only by a few bright green leaden roofs and a pair of large church domes rising from its medieval kremlin.

The sun has retreated behind grey-white clouds. We go back to our places. The soup kettle is late today so we have to gnaw on rusks, of which everyone has brought along several sacks. The pails are not distributed until about four in the afternoon. Then the train rolls on.

Westward! So it won't be Archangel after all, which lies another five hundred kilometers due north. The only other way we can reach Kotlas, which the transport leader has named as our rail destination, is through Vyatka.[4] The river route along the Sukhona is out of the question at this time of year.

Again the forest looms up on both sides. Day by day we are feeling more isolated, in spite of our numerous company. We try to strike up conversations but after a few sentences they usually die. Having a smoke helps a little to relieve the monotony. With deliberate fuss I roll myself cigarettes out of cheap stem tobacco and pieces of newspaper. In spite of the cold and the agonizing hunger pangs, we feel weary. Those who manage to stay warm enough are able to get some sleep.

Half dozing I begin my mental writing again. Events, people, long forgotten places—all press for attention. My memory is as full as my stomach is empty . . ..

Before me I see the village cemetery in Mariental. The rusty iron gate closes gently behind me. I am walking along neatly raked paths bordered by tall shrubs and grasses. I am familiar with every grave here, every tree. Under the birch over there, its broad branches waving languorously in the evening breeze, lie the remains of my ancestors who had first come to this country from Prussia. I never knew them, of course, but one of their sayings brought them alive for me and my generation. "Russia is our way, not our homeland," they had always maintained. As a child, I associated their words with the difficult pioneer years of the last century.

I see myself as a child again on the summer evening when I first heard that somber proverb. The sun is sinking to a blue horizon far behind the meadow beyond the river. Overhead the dry birch branches whisper and I proudly

[4]This settlement was renamed Kirov in 1934.

clasp Grandfather's huge forefinger as we stand over the graves. I glance up at the soft cloud of white beard, the mild eyes gazing into the distance. Later, I would often study that face in the yellowed photograph in our parlor.

"Russia is our way . . . our long way," Grandfather says loudly. "That is what my father used to say, and his father before him. By the 'way' they meant the Anabaptist way of life handed down to us by our forefathers and by God's Word in the New Testament. Never forget that, Sasha. Our people came here a long, long time ago—over a hundred years ago. And still we are only guests in this land. This is our home for now, but it can never be our homeland."

Clack—clack-clack—clack—clack-clack. The wheels keep sounding their weary burden. I am dragged out of my childhood reverie back into the sullen present.

Day and night crawl after each other hypnotically. Only a child crying out with cold or hunger disturbs the leaden journey. When we address a neighbor it is to get rid for a moment of unendurable feelings of loneliness. Even Ohm Peters, whom no one ever sees upset or depressed, is retreating into silence.

We reach Vyatka on the twenty-seventh of October. For a whole day our train is left standing on a siding. When mealtime comes, instead of the pail being handed in, the side door is pushed open noisily.

"Make room in there!" bawls Fur Cap, his face lobster-red as he pushes up to us a Russian priest in a shabby fur coat. The priest, a little disheveled, stands up, bows deeply in the Russian manner and, as a blessing, smoothly makes the sign of the cross to left and right.

"Thirty-four," Tielmann gives the count.

We are still not over our surprise when a Mennonite countryman swings into the car with his pack. He is followed slowly by his obviously pregnant wife, who groans heavily as he pulls her up. The door rumbles shut.

"Count!" yells the leader.

"Thirty-five, thirty-six," Tielmann resumes the count. "This must be the first departure from schedule," he adds.

The train gets under way abruptly. The Albrecht lad who is sitting on the big wooden chest loses his balance and his legs fly up in the air. His grandfather chuckles and turns to the Mennonite newcomer.

"*Woa senn je hea?*" (Where are you from?) he inquires affably in Low German.

"*Ut Oreburg*" (from Orenburg)[5] the man replies. He looks astonished. "*Woat, je senn uck Dietsche?*" (What, you're German too?) he adds.

His wife, plainly delighted, beams from under the thick folds of her kerchief.

---

[5]Orenburg, a daughter colony of the Old Colony in South Russia, was established on the Ural River in Eastern European Russian in 1892-93 and consisted of some twenty-five villages with a total pre-war population of some five thousand.

"John Bergen," the newcomer says, in High German this time, "from Suvorovka."[6]

With this laconic introduction our acquaintance is sealed. The women survey the pregnant woman with sympathy and make room for her on a bunk. Bergen sits down on his bundle.

The priest stands there demurely, his back against the door. He has a pale, thin face around which is molded a thick, grey beard. His deep-set eyes are direct and warm.

"Have you come far, Little Father?" I invite him with my hand to sit down beside me.

"From Samara[7], my son," he says with typical Russian cordiality. "Father Nikolai." His voice is soft and melodious and his beard stirs when he speaks.

He smiles. "Please accept me into your suffering family; we are all traveling the same road."

Bergen is now telling his story to those nearest him, with his wife occasionally interrupting to correct a detail. They speak in what is for them the more familiar Low German. I catch the well-worn word "*kulak*" from time to time; the wife pronounces it with the inimitable accent of Mennonite colonists' wives whose Russian is limited.

I remain unmoved; it's always the same story: Chekist secret police, night arrests, then the cruel miles across the cold steppe. The women express their sympathies through awkward interruptions. Who among them has not had similar experiences, I reflect; but here a stranger's grief is felt as deeply as one's own misfortunes. Mrs. Bergen describes in detail their three-week transport from Orenburg to Vyatka: the door of their boxcar, for example, had never once been opened even though the corpse of a man who had died on the way had lain in the corner almost the entire time. As she relives the sorrowful experience the tears flow again. Father Nikolai appears to follow the gist of the account from the facial expressions and the tears; he crosses himself and his lips move silently.

Our train stops in Vyatka for a day and a half. Then the swaying and the silence begin again. The wheels roll out their melody and beat their steady tempo on the rails. The men rise wordlessly in order to warm themselves by swinging their arms. Then they sit down again.

Some kind of human communication is essential I feel. I begin a conversation with the priest and ask the inevitable question: Why? When? Where?

"Well, of course, this is a time of exile, my son," he begins carefully, then looks at me appraisingly. "That's quite according to Scripture—yes. Persecution has again become the mark of a Christian, as it was in the ancient church. Nowadays one arouses suspicion if one is not persecuted for one's

[6]A village on the western border of the Orenburg settlement. Orenburg is one of the few Mennonite settlements in Soviet Russia which has survived almost intact to the present time.

[7]This province was located on the Volga immediately west of Orenburg.

faith. And even now it will not be in vain." He drops his voice almost to a whisper: "Our Russian people will awake, believe me, they will awake." He rocks himself as if in confirmation and as he nods his leonine head his long hair cascades forward over his shoulders.

"Yes," I say, relieved to hear a human voice again.

He grows talkative. "For eighteen years I served a village congregation near Kazan. And how much suffering I saw! Our people are poor and ailing. But the question of God, you know, is far more important than the question of land. Then there is the drunkenness, the brutality—but all that suffering is merely training for the hereafter.

"An old peasant woman came to see me one day. 'Little Father,' she said, 'my old man is dying; he always came to church—you know that—but he liked his drink. He's got little time left. Can you come tomorrow, or the day after?' So I went. He was lying on the couch weeping, the way he always did after a night of debauchery during which he had beaten his wife, who was quite used to such degradation. At such times he would kneel early in the morning for hours before the icon. At early mass he would sing in his rolling bass from the choir loft. What a voice he had. His *'Gospodi pomilui'* Lord have mercy, came out of the depths of a guilt-ridden soul."

The priest is losing himself in details, but I listen to him gratefully.

"So now he confessed his black life, took communion, and died—died comforted in God's name. He was like a thief in this." The priest looks at me gravely. "We are a nation of spiritual thieves." Again he leans towards me, as if confiding a secret: "And what if these times finally change us from spiritual thieves into real disciples?"

He is too moved to continue; he heaves a sigh and once more taps his cross: *"Gospodi pomilui."*

Outside, the forest looms ever taller and thicker. We are traveling through giant stands of birch; the slender white trunks shimmer past the window. Koehn observes them for a long time through a crack in the door. When he looks up he catches my gaze.

"What riches our country possesses," he exclaims with wonder in his voice as he picks his way towards me through the baggage.

"Then again maybe it's poor, Koehn, bitterly poor." I answer, "because it has so many poor people—or because it has such a tragic destiny." I yawn. "We'll never see the sun again, old Peter. From now on we'll be sitting in shadows . . . ."

"Archangel?" He drops the name between us for the first time.

"And even if it isn't Archangel, who can survive by the polar sea?"

He nods and looks grim. "You know, Sasha, this whole scene . . ." he indicates the huddled figures around us. "If our forefathers could see it." His hand comes down on my arm. "Would they still think their flight to the Russian steppes worthwhile?" He rubs his chilled hands together thoughtfully. "And those still at home, on the collective, will go our way too. After this winter nothing will ever grow for us again, my friend."

Our conversation is interrupted by Koehn's oldest son, Willie, the fourteen-year-old, who leaps to his feet with a cry. He shouts something and keeps grabbing at his foot with his mittened hands. His mother pulls off his felt boot. The foot is white as marble. With Willie wincing and whimpering in her ear, she gently massages it for awhile and then wraps it with more rags, which she pulls out of a bundle. The boy sobs himself to sleep.

The incident makes us all restless. There is a general stirring as we knock our feet together, stretch our arms, and slap ourselves warm on chest and shoulders.

Next day our pailful of gruel fails to arrive on time. During our few stops Fur Cap stays close to the baggage car. At one stop the crew load birch wood into the extra cars while the locomotive pants noisily. Neufeld tries yelling out the peephole but nobody pays any attention.

In the afternoon the children start complaining. They are hungry.

"Right away," Mrs. Koehn tries to soothe her brood.

"Soon, soon. Now hush," says Mrs. Albrecht. Even we adults are becoming impatient. Around four o'clock the women produce rusks from the sacks; the children crunch them with chattering teeth.

According to my calendar on the side of the boxcar we have been underway for almost a week and a half since leaving Moscow. We should be arriving in Kotlas anytime now. And it won't be a moment too soon. This half-starved existence, cooped up and freezing in a swaying boxcar, is becoming an unendurable torture. How we long just to set our feet on solid ground again, to be out of this claustrophobic cage.

But the days and nights keep repeating themselves, the birches and pines keep racing past the peephole, and the wheels underneath keep up their clatter.

I observe that we younger men, who had been clean-shaven, have grown an assortment of beards. It's amazing, but beards have an oddly independent character. I mean, you can't tell from a man's face and head what kind of beard he will sprout. Koehn, for example, with his broad, masculine face and head, has a little blond beard that grows to a delicate point. Tielmann, on the other hands, has a tiny head and narrow face, but his beard is a wide, lusty tangle of black curls. Our foreheads, cheeks, and hands are black with grime. We have had no water for washing since Moscow. But no one registers distaste or repugnance. People forced to endure cold and hunger are not likely to be squeamish about dirt and smells.

Abruptly during the night of November first, while making a stop at a wood-loading station, we hear a couple of shots. The echoes roll through the forest like exploding cannon shells. The women are terrified.

"To hell with them," comes the thundering voice of the transport leader. "Let them rot here, the thieving bastards."

Koehn's guess is that two members of the crew must have broken into the supply car.

I recall how year after year I tried to bring the geography of this region alive for my students. Now I am myself part of this remote geography, traveling through Vologda, Vyatka, and heaven knows where else. And what has happened to my boys? After I was dismissed from my teaching post three years ago (no reason given) and put to work on the collective, I lost track of many of them. Most of them will have to make the hard choice between serving in the Red army or making excursions of the kind we are making. And if they do come this way will they remember the flora and fauna of the Far North? Will they remember the school and me? Perhaps they'll have to learn to forget even themselves, like the rest of us. In the face of our grim circumstances here I feel sorry for them already.

How did the lesson go again? Ah yes, this region is the home of the Zyrians[8] or, as they call themselves, the Komi. They are a sub-race of a quarter of a million, all told. I can recall the illustrations in our textbook clearly: two short, powerful-looking figures with oval, Finnish-type faces who live by hunting, fishing, cottage industry, and a little farming. Great Russians have settled here in the North also, with most of them settling in the region around Archangel. That about exhausts my knowledge of the region.

I see that it is beginning to snow again. The flakes swirling through the peephole cover Ohm Peters' fur cap with a fine white film. He is asleep. I get up and close the opening. But the snow continues to crumble through the seams and cracks in the walls; garish white specks penetrate ever more deeply into the car. Tielmann wakes up with a start. I wave my arm to indicate that we are being infiltrated. He laughs, thrusts his shapeless mitt into his capacious pocket and stiffly pulls out a copy of *Pravda*, the official state paper. "Let *Truth*," he says grandly, "protect us!" He slaps his arms around his shoulders a few times, throws his mitts on a box, blows on his reddened hands, and carefully presses sheets of *Pravda* into the cracks behind his back.

By next morning the snowstorm is even worse. The pail of buckwheat gruel, thin though it is, performs a minor miracle today. It not only warms us up but actually revives us. Slowly we thaw out and begin to talk again.

As usual, Ohm Peters gives us the benediction of his warm, solacing presence. The women are preoccupied with the needs of the children. We younger men are restless and on edge. Tielmann in particular is fed up with the tedium. He feels the need for some kind of emotional release.

"Little Father," he turns to the priest half facetiously, as though trying to provoke him, "even you have to admit that our situation is looking worse all the time."

"It's bad my son," Father Nikolai agrees calmly, "but we have a proverb: Without God you can't step across the threshold, with Him you can step across the ocean. Yes . . . but tell me something. Where do all of you come from?"

"We're German-Mennonite colonists from the Saratov region. As you can

---

[8]These are a Finnic people living in the northeastern U.S.S.R. They are divided into the Zyrians and the Permyaks. Both branches of Komi speak a Finno-Permian language and now have a combined population of five-hundred thousand.

see we've been given our traveling papers. There isn't much else to tell."
Tielmann waves his hand in dismissal. "It's always the same story."

"Aha—German? Colonists?" the priest echoes in surprise. "Well, well, so
that's what you all are? And you too? You speak a good Russian."

"Yes, I'm German too, but I had the opportunity to learn a little more Russian, in preparation for becoming a village teacher."

"A teacher? Ah, yes, well that explains it then." He nods his head vigorously. "Yes, well . . . now we know—." He continues to nod vigorously and
screws up his eyes.

For a few moments there is silence. The priest looks down thoughtfully at
his sleeves, which he has shoved into each other for warmth.

"It's tedious to sit like this." He looks up hopefully. "You, Mr. Teacher,
perhaps you could tell us a story?"

Tielmann sits up. "Tell you a story? All right. Perhaps a literary piece?"

"A literary piece," the priest agrees eagerly. Most of our great writers, at
one time or another, were exiles too. Pushkin, Lermontov, Gogol . . . the list
goes on and on—Turgenev, Dostoyevsky, even the great Lev Tolstoy, in a
sense. I'm sure any and all of them have something by way of consolation to
offer us here—."

"Yes, yes," Tielmann interrupts, excited now, "you're right, Father, they
were all exiles too." He is in his element. "But here—I'll give you something
from a modern writer. Do you know Ehrenburg?"[9]

Father Nikolai's face registers consternation. "Ilya Ehrenburg the—?"

"—that's right, the Antichrist," Tielmann prompts impatiently. "But early
in his career he wrote very differently, as in his *Prayer for Russia*. And what
a prayer it is!"

He waves his arms enthusiastically. "You know, during my last year as a
teacher we presented it at a parents' night. It's in the style of the Orthodox
mass and sung in four parts . . .. Don't be offended Father," he suddenly
pleads. "But, as you can imagine, our audience at that time was completely
divided in their reception of it. Half of them took it for what it is, a genuine
prayer, while the *komsomol*[10] members interpreted it as a satire on the Russian Church and punctuated the performance with hoots of derision. At first I
was tempted to put those fellows in their places, but I realized that such an
action could lead to unpleasant consequences for the school. In the end we
sang it for both heaven and hell! It may even be that the scoffing of those
youths saved our freedom that day . . .. If you wish I'll recite it for you."

Tielmann stands erect and formal, his sensitive face demanding attention.
That's exactly the way he used to look in his classroom. In his massive fur
coat, tall and serious, there is something symbolically Russian about him. He

[9]Ilya Ehrenburg (1891-1967) was a journalist and novelist who spent many years in
the West (1929-40) and thus became the most cosmopolitan of Soviet writers. While a
skilled propagandist for the Soviet regime, he is best known for his novel *The Thaw*
(1954), which heralded the more relaxed post-Stalinist period officially announced by
Khrushchev in 1956.

[10]These are members of the Communist Union of Youths, a Soviet organization for
young people of sixteen and over.

throws out his right arm in a dramatic gesture and begins to recite in the voice of a dissolute village commissar.

> Hey, forget your ancient woes,
> It's time to live it up!
> We're fired up by
> Splendid resolutions! declarations!
> Hey, my darling, how about it?
> —You're playing hard to get?
> Look, we won't give up—
> A kiss—or else you'll get . . .
> A bullet, or a bayonet . . .
> Yes, loudly night and day
> We'll celebrate our liberty!

Father Nikolai, embarrassed, stares straight ahead. Tielmann is too engrossed in his performance to notice. "Now here's the chorus," he explains. In his fine, rich baritone he begins to chant in the style and rhythm of the Orthodox mass (he has obviously studied its form carefully).

> For our country, our motherland,
> Let us pray in *peace to God.*

Tielmann elevates his tone appropriately on the final syllables.

> For our fields, lying barren and bleak,
> For our unloving hearts,
> For those who cannot pray,
> For those who strangle children,
> For those singing joyless songs,
> For those wielding knives and spears,
> And for those who howl like dogs,
> Let us pray in *peace to God.*

Again he raises his voice and draws the last phrase out resonantly. Then he steps back and in a voice vibrating with passion declaims:

> Lord, your land lies naked and drunk,
> Your vast domain.
> It sought release from sorrows
> Through riotous celebration.
> Now it groans in the mire . . ..

The voice softens into pathos:

> Once there was an infinite measure
> Of prayer for all who suffered pain.
> And the faithful sought through prayer
> To spread the cross to people everywhere.
> They gazed towards the silent East,
> To the hills, the snow, the spring;
> And they spoke through tears of faith:
> 'Look there . . . the land of Christ!'
> Then new life was brought by prayer—
> But now it is no longer there . . ..

And again the solemn chant:
> For all the many graves,
> Let us pray in *peace to God!*
> For those who still bear crosses,
> For those bereft of cross and stone;
> For the broken stone that was a church,
> For the lamps unlit, for bells untolled;
> For all desolation triumphant,
> Let us pray in *peace to God!*

Father Nikolai has raised his head and is gazing wistfully at the speaker. Tielmann delivers the closing section in a low intense voice.
> Lord, forgive us, have pity,
> Do not forsake us in death.
> We have lived all—and lost all;
> Lift us up from the mire
> To you, the Three-in-One . . ..
> Let this evil life explode
> The spirit's heavy chains;
> So that with ardent glances
> It may win Your lighter burden;
> So that with purging grief,
> It may redeem this living hell.
> Let it taste other joys:
> Penitence and honest labor.
> Life which now in error strays,
> Lord, forgive our sinful ways!
> So that our sun may shine again
> O'er white churches, sky-blue domes,
> And Russia on her knees again . . ..
> For Russia—
> Let us pray in *peace to God.*

Tielmann sits down amidst respectful silence. His pent-up emotions expended, he looks more relaxed. For a few moments there is complete silence, except for the clack—clack of the wheels. Father Nikolai has thrust his long-maned head into his hands. He is muttering to himself.

During Tielmann's performance the children have awakened. Several of the women stare uncomprehendingly at the teacher. Their glances plainly say that they think he has gone crazy. But no one says a word. The men's faces are expressionless, but they no doubt recall that daring performance in the village school. How long ago it seems!

Early next morning—it's hardly dawn—I am awakened by a piercing cry. Another accident? But the boxcar keeps on rocking without letup. Another terrifying scream—a woman's voice—in our car! I hear an exchange of whispers. Ohm Peters and Mrs. Koehn vacate their places. The Orenburger, Bergen, is bending over his wife's bunk in the corner. Now I understand. Poor woman. The husband and Ohm Peters stand together with their backs to the bunk while Mrs. Koehn tends the woman in labor.

Her cries grow even more penetrating. Bergen stands there helpless, his face like chalk. His drained features work desperately as he fights for control. The scene is becoming uncomfortable. Several angry children's voices rise to meet the screams in the corner. Then the children fall silent as the woman continues to groan loudly and thrash her arms against the wall. I stick my thumbs in my ears and squeeze my eyes shut. Still I hear everything and my eyes fly open involuntarily. Oh, my Liese, Liese, that's how your screams once pierced my soul, until you had no more screams left and I was hurt beyond all grief.

Bergen's faded cheeks are wet and he keeps blinking his eyes. He can't stand anymore. Forgetting that he is acting as a screen he goes to the peephole, sticks out his head and begins to scream. But his desperate cries are muffled by the rumble of wind and train. The cries echo·faintly, as though from a remote distance.

Bergen's face is a deep red when he turns from the peephole. In a rage he leaps at the door and treads on Willie Koehn, who begins to moan piteously. Bergen jerks frantically at the door handle, but the door does not budge. He keeps on pulling and pushing, and with every futile exertion emits a strange animal noise. I begin to sweat . . ..

The wavering filament of an infant's voice! Like a wild beast Bergen turns and flings himself into the corner. I glimpse a blur of grey linen rags, then a bundled, blood-soaked shawl is pushed through the window. Mrs. Albrecht gets up and silently edges her father out of the way. The women wrap and bind and speak rapidly to each other. The turbulent moments seem to go on and on. I whip my fur collar over my head and close my eyes again.

When I look up some time later, the young mother lies asleep on her bunk. Her haggard face looks like a death mask. The infant is asleep too. The rest sit close together, dozing or conversing casually, as though nothing had happened.

On the fifth of November we reach Kotlas in the midst of a blinding snowstorm. Although we arrive in the small hours of the morning, the car doors are not opened until seven o'clock.

We are uncertain and apprehensive about what awaits us here, but relieved that the fatiguing confinement of the train is over at last. Bergen timidly approaches the transport leader to see if he can get some kind of special treatment for his sick wife. But Fur Cap dismisses him with the crude remark that we have not been sent here for breeding purposes and goes on his way.

Kotlas is situated at the confluence of the Sukhona and the Vychegda Rivers, at the very source of the Northern Dvina which flows into the White Sea farther north. These northern rivers have frozen over long ago. The railway network ends here at Kotlas. If they intend to send us farther north, they will have to do it by sleigh. At least our movements will be free then; we'll be able to walk and run to overcome the cold. The others press around

Tielmann and me: "What'll happen? Where to?" We tell them we don't know. There is no point in scaring them with our premonitions.

The station is flooded with people. The forlorn crowds of exiles already here seem to be waiting for further orders. Emaciated men and boys are wandering around on the platform outside. They look like Russians from the south. Even more pitiful-looking creatures are sitting or squatting around the entrance. In the close, putrid-smelling waiting room dozens of women and children are lying huddled together on the messy floor. Two young girls are standing beside a bench near the door, quietly watching their dying mother. A pale and uncomplaining skeleton, a victim of tuberculosis beyond any doubt, the woman lies there, her eyes already fixed in a death-stare, dribbling words too faint to be heard.

I turn and find myself facing an unbelievably shriveled old peasant who is holding out a crooked, trembling hand.

"For the love of Christ," he wheezes, "a piece of bread, sir!"

When I try to avert my face his eyes widen in alarm. "We're starving here, comrade—for the fifth day—after coming all the long way from Ekaterinoslav."

His thin face is grotesque with swellings and lumps and he has a loathsome breath. I extract a piece of rusk from my coat pocket. He tears it greedily from my hand, makes a shaky sign of the cross, and hobbles off.

Kotlas is an isolated little market town. From the station it looks drab and miserably poor. The only touches of color are a few red flags, made of silk, of course! There are some brick buildings dominating the irregular rows of primitive wooden huts. There is also the inevitable church bell tower, but I notice that the bell is missing . . ..

As we did in Moscow, the four hundred of us are ordered to line up on the station platform. The sky hangs over us like an old grey kettle. From it the snowflakes spiral down thickly, incessantly. With limbs stiffened up from the cold and the confinement, we stand there beside our belongings feeling clumsy and heavy, as though wearing leg-irons. The new mother, bundled into her husband's fur coat, almost smothers her piteously wailing infant in her attempts to keep it warm.

Fur Cap is dashing around calling out names from his grubby list. This time the roll-call appears to be proceeding without incident, although as usual the man doesn't spare even the women and children the grossest abuse and curses.

Some members of the older transport try to slip into our group. But the guards keep a sharp watch and roughly chase the intruders away.

A Red Guard shouts to us in passing that thirty sleighs have been ordered for us. No one thinks to ask him when they are coming.

So we wait, a heavy lethargy settling over us again.

In the afternoon it stops snowing but gets much colder. Ragged strands of hoarfrost dangle from our beards. The faces of the women and children look pinched and numb under the snow-laden folds of their babushkas. Some of us can't bear the freezing immobility any longer. We start running around—more like staggering, really—beating our arms and felt boots together, but it doesn't help much. We are so chilled through we can't stop shivering.

"Koehn," I call out in desperation, "grab a hold; we'll carry our boxes up and down—that'll warm us up."

Koehn grabs one end and laboriously we half-drag half-carry our biggest box up and down. It's a shock to discover how the fatigue and poor diet of the past month have weakened us. But we do manage to warm up a little.

Ohm Peters is rubbing his grandson's bare foot with snow. At first the boy bawls with pain, but after a while he is actually laughing. It's good to hear laughter again, especially a child's laughter.

The short northern day is already glimmering when the first sleighs arrive. They are the usual peasant type, open at the back and shallow. We used such sleighs on our farms to haul logs for firewood. They consist of two sturdy runners attached to wooden crosspieces and a rough wooden floor with a bundle of straw on top. One skinny nag is hitched to each sleigh between crooked shafts under a curved wooden yoke. A few of the sleighs have peasant boys as drivers, but most of them are driverless and, in the Russian manner, simply follow the lead sleigh.

Quickly, in sheer relief, we load our boxes and bundles and help the women and children into the sleighs. We men prefer to walk.

Fur Cap occupies the lead sleigh. The other guards distribute themselves through the train. The lead driver shouts *"Poshol!"* and the trek begins. The bony-hipped horses throw themselves against the ragged traces. I note we are heading northwest.

We are breaking trail in snow that is well over half a meter deep everywhere. Just beyond Kotlas we reach the monotonous tundra landscape so characteristic of this region. It is an uneven, marshy plain. Between low moss hummocks I catch the sparkle of ice, which means in summer the roads must be impassable. Far up ahead the forest shimmers blue as we slowly move towards it. Glancing back I see how the forest bends in and around Kotlas like a gigantic green saber.

It's a great relief to be able to walk freely again. But after a couple of hours we feel extremely weary. For a while the children run alongside us, but they soon tire and climb back into the sleighs.

At one point we pass the mutilated cadaver of a horse; it is surrounded by fresh wolf tracks. A huge raven is perched on the carcass and stubbornly refuses to be driven off.

"I'll wager it's minus thirty degrees," Ohm Peters pants as he vigorously rubs his whitening earlobes. Our feet are reasonably warm from walking, but our wind-exposed upper bodies are shuddering with cold. To make things worse, there is the ever-present ache of hunger aggravated by the exertion of walking in the open. We keep sucking and gnawing our frozen rusks, but they don't help much.

As the snow gets deeper, the road gets softer. The semi-darkness of a northern night has thickened the white landscape to an eerie grey murk. The monotonous slishing of the sleigh runners sounds more muffled now. The thin but trail-wise nags struggle through the snow at a steady pace. Somewhere a child complains and a mother soothes in the darkness.

The earlier snatches of conversation have ceased. Each of us is preoccupied now only with himself, with the grim reality of plodding step by step through this frozen wasteland to a destination unknown and unimaginable. We don't know its location or shape yet, but we do know that it lies waiting to receive us in its iron embrace. And when we reach it, I think gloomily, Russia will cease to be just a "way" for us and will become our "home" at last—our final home here on earth.

Around eleven in the evening a light appears in the snow wastes on one side of the forest. Bergen is the first to spot it and gives me a nudge. We stare at it like exhausted swimmers in sight of land.

But distances are deceptive out in the open. It takes another full hour for our train to arrive at a miserable-looking little village. Lackluster rays of light filter out into the streets from the tiny wooden huts.

We slump down on the edge of our sleigh sick with exhaustion. After Fur Cap has inspected several of the huts, he gives the drivers a few curt instructions and they scatter among the yards.

Our sleigh is sent to the most outlying huts on the edge of the village. Ohm Peters stays with his family; the Koehns, the Neufelds, and the Penners remain together too. Father Nikolai, who had ridden in our sleigh during the last part of the trek, joins the Bergens and me in the last hut.

An almost suffocating wave of heat hits us as we enter. The young mother collapses on the threshold. We lay her carefully on the low bench running along one wall; then Bergen places the infant in its wrappings on the warm top of the large brick oven.

The hut consists of one dim, shabby room. From the raw beam that runs across the blackened ceilings hangs a rusty little lamp. It has an oily smell. A huge, charred wedge of pine-resin has been stuck into one wall; it must serve frequently as a substitute for the precious lamp. A double sheet of newspaper serves as a pane in the only window.

An old woman with sunken cheeks but warm eyes emerges from the dark corner beside the stove. Her toothless jaws clamped firmly together, she inspects us with the directness of the elderly.

"*Zdrastvuite!*" she greets us heartily. "Have you come from far?" She cups a hand over one ear as she speaks.

"From Moscow, Grandmother!" Bergen's voice sounds loud in the tiny room.

The old woman looks alarmed.

I try to reassure her. "*Nichevo,* it's nothing, we're friendly people." I smile encouragingly and turn to Father Nikolai. "You know, it's always been like that. When has the Russian peasant not feared Moscow?" The priest smiles and nods in agreement.

When the old crone sees the priest all her uneasiness vanishes. She follows him to the corner where an ikon of the Savior is hanging on the wall with a small red lamp flickering over it. Father Nikolai prays fervently for a few moments. Then he turns to the woman and gives her and her house a blessing. His deeply reverential manner brings a glow of ecstasy to her withered face. It is probably a long time since she has had a priest in her home.

"Sit down, Little Father, sit down my darlings," she bubbles and breaks into tremulous coughing.

"I'll get the samovar ready for you," she shrills between coughs and bustles around wheezing and sputtering.

Twenty minutes later the humming samovar stands on the table. What a beautiful sound, and how long since I've heard it. The old woman sets three earless cups on the table and fetches a piece of black bread from the pantry. While Bergen tends to his wife, the priest and I greedily start sipping the hot tea. We tear off chunks of bread and wash them down with noisy gulps of tea.

Gradually I get feeling back in my feet. As my body warms up, I am suffused with a feeling of sheer bliss. The bread has disappeared down to the last crumb, the samovar is empty. Suddenly I feel giddy as my whole being relaxes in a way that has become unfamiliar. I drape my fur coat over the floor and stretch out on it with a sight of contentment.

Early next morning our train forges ahead again. The food, warmth, and rest have done us a world of good. Our joints still ache but we feel mentally and physically refreshed.

We finally reach the forest and find a new northern world opening up to us, but one no less forbidding. The snow is even deeper here and every step is a labor in itself. Even the frozen marsh puddles are drifted over. Only the tall pines glimmer red-brown and dark green in this white world. There is no sign of life anywhere. Then high in a tree top a solitary woodpecker strikes up a percussive beat. The sound is reassuring.

The small horses have an even tougher time of it today, as they are forced to drag the sleighs over completely unbroken trails. Clouds of steam rise from their backs and flanks as they plough their way through the drifts between the massive tree trunks. It's distressing to watch them. We try to ease our own way by stepping with painful precision in the awkwardly trampled footsteps of the lead men.

So our progress today is slower than ever. It doesn't take long before the horses begin to slow their pace. Their backs are dark wet stains and their legs, manes, nostrils, and tails are spangled with hoarfrost and icicles. The visible parts of the trees are also festooned with fantastic garlands of frost. I am overcome by a curious feeling of unreality, as though any moment now we will all, horses and people, stop moving and stand here like the trees, frozen forever into weird shapes of arctic petrifaction.

My glance snags on something beside the trail. It's a torn felt boot sticking out of a white mound. I look over at Koehn; he has noticed the snow-covered corpse too.

In the late afternoon a wind springs up and snow begins to swirl down so thickly that Fur Cap is forced to halt the train; he orders the sleighs to form up in several half-circles. It's not any concession to us, of course; he fears that we might lose our way and that the horses might play out before night. Nevertheless, we are grateful even for an indirect mercy. Fur Cap surprises us even more by allowing bread to be distributed from the sack in the lead sleigh. It turns out to be both frozen and bitter, but we are glad to have it.

Our stop lasts about half an hour, although Fur Cap starts cursing and threatening impatiently long before that. But it's been long enough to allow the horses and us to recover our strength a little. Fortunately, the wind and snow have let up somewhat too. Whips swinging, the drivers shout at their nags and our train reluctantly reassembles itself for the last lap of the day. We drag along for another hour or so—northward, always farther north.

Next day Ohm Peters begins to lag behind. In desperation he pulls himself onto the back of the rear sleigh. The nag flounders, unable to take the extra weight, and comes to an awkward halt. We try to get it moving, but all it can manage is a terrified sideways lurch which collapses it into the snow. There is nothing we can do but wait and give the exhausted horse time to recover. Finally, with an almost superhuman effort we manage to get horse and sleigh back on the tracks.

The rest of the train has not stopped for us and is already far ahead. It stretches along the white wastes like a crooked black branch. I spot a fox spoor beside the trail, the only sign I have seen that any animals exist in this frozen white hell.

We continue in this way for five agonizing days. Snow, fatigue, hunger, and curses, make up a round only briefly interrupted by the welcome nights in the miserable Zyrian villages where our train stops and commandeers the huts. The villagers—sometimes friendly, sometimes not—give us the hot tea and dry bread which give us enough strength to send us on our way the next morning. During the day we are forced to make numerous rest stops. At one point, just when we are on the verge of collapse, we are shocked into further exertion by the sight of a snow-covered rig which with horse and driver has been buried in this boundless graveyard of ice and snow. The terror pulses through our tired brains as we picture ourselves frozen into similar grotesque statues. And our terror gives us the extra energy that keeps driving us along, kilometer after kilometer. The world around us may be dead, but we have not lost our desire to live.

The stark polarities of our thoughts and feelings are separated by vast continents of silent exertion. We have little to say to each other, even at night in the huts. It's as though we have become disembodied from each other, become separate atoms floating alone and silent and aimless in a void. Ohm Peters was right: we are losing all sense of time and space here in the North. From day to day the hard details of our journey dissolve in our consciousness with the swiftness of a dream after waking.

When one day we finally reach our destination on the far side of the Mezen River, not one of us can recall clearly how this miracle has come about.

Part Two
Our Bitter Bread

But the father of all [industry] is our Russian forest with its genuinely golden tree trunks (gold is mined from them), and the oldest of all the kinds of work in the Archipelago is logging. It summons everyone to itself and has room for everyone, and it is not even out of bounds for cripples (they will send out a three-man gang of armless men to stamp down the foot and-a-half of snow) . . .. You are a lumberjack. First you yourself stamp it down next to the tree trunk. You cut down the tree. Then, hardly able to make your way through the snow, you cut off all the branches (and you have to feel them out in the snow and get to them with your ax). Still dragging your way through the same loose snow, you have to carry off all the branches and make piles of them and burn them. (They smoke. They don't burn.) And now you have to saw up the wood to size and stack it. And the work norm for you and your brother for the day is six and a half cubic yards each, or thirteen cubic yards for two men working together . . ..

You come to hate the forest, this beauty of the earth, whose praises have been sung in verse and prose. You come to walk beneath the arches of pines and birch with a shudder of revulsion!
—Aleksandr I. Solzhenitsyn,
The Gulag Archipelago Two, pp. 199-200

Deep in the vast pine forest we arrive at a compound consisting of a dozen dilapidated wooden barracks, each measuring about six by twenty-five meters: a wall down the middle divides each of them into halves. After looking around Koehn and I walk over to the farthest one and inspect it through the doorway. There is no ceiling: the bare board roof is full of gaping cracks and is sagging in the middle where the weight of snow is heaviest. The long cracks have admitted snow into the interior which is furnished only with tiers of rough plank bunks warped and weathered in crazy angles of disrepair. These barracks must have been built for forest workers who have long since disappeared—God knows where. Were they swallowed up by this silent, ruthless beast of a forest? If so, it must have been a long time ago. Everything appears decayed from long neglect. The window openings, a meter and a half wide and a meter high, have been nailed shut with boards. The floor consists of bare, well-trodden earth. In the center stands a large brick stove smeared over in a makeshift way with clay. At least we'll enjoy some warmth again, if we can close up the worst of the cracks.

"So this is Camp Number 513," I say grimly to Koehn.

"Just as you ordered it, my dear sirs and voluntary settlers!" The loud, hearty voice behind us startles us. "Enter, please, enter and make yourselves at home!"

The voice sounds like a ghost from the past. Before me stands a tall, thin fellow with a long, narrow face and a black, curly beard dividing sharply at the chin-cleft. He is about my own age. I know that sardonic voice and those mocking eyes. I look at him more closely. It can't be.

"Not Waldemar Wolff, from Saratov?" I blurt out in amazement.

"The one and—" Now he recognizes me too. "Alexander? The eternal optimist from Mariental? I don't believe it. So you've landed here too? And just now? We were in the same transport and didn't know it."

He can't seem to stop pumping my hand. "It's too much of a coincidence," he rambles on happily. "Our highly efficient socialist system simply doesn't allow for such chance encounters. Somebody must have slipped up. Reunions between intellectuals and dissenters like us are forbidden. Somebody will pay for this. Heads will roll!"

I can't get in a word. He's the same irrepressible, gibing Volodya Wolff. "But Wolff," I finally manage, "what are you doing here, man? You of all people. I would have thought with your wanderlust you'd have skipped the country long ago."

"I did Sasha, I did, but I came back again—couldn't stay away from our Red Paradise. I'll tell you about it sometime." He pauses; the old lop-sided grin flashes. "What? With my name don't you think I fit right into this idyllic northern hunting ground?"

For the first time in months I find myself laughing spontaneously, in sheer delight. Finding Wolff here is like finding a diamond in a manure pile.

He grabs my arm. "All right, Sasha, this is where we'll play house now. I'll get my stuff from the other barrack and we'll move in together. We'll live and play together as we did when we sat together in high school. After all, we've moved up to the University of the North now. What do you say?"

Our first job is to light a fire so we can thaw out at last. We break off dry pine branches and drag them into the barrack. The children lay claim to the second and third levels of the bunks. Several of them suffer minor falls as rotten boards succumb to the unaccustomed weight. Boxes and chests are forced open amidst much creaking and scraping so the women can get out the required bedclothes and other things. Then they move over to the stove to warm themselves and their bedding. For the night we hang our fur coats across the badly boarded windows. Tomorrow we will have to do some repair work to make our new home habitable.

We are all together again—Koehn, Peters, Neufeld, Penner, and their families. Even Father Nikolai has contrived to stay with our group. He takes a bunk near Tielmann, Wolff, and me. Wolff immediately dubs our area "bachelor's corner."

Two old barn lanterns hanging from the ceiling give us a barely adequate lighting system. After Wolff has fetched his stuff from the other barrack we lie on our bunks for a while smoking and reminiscing about the past. How glad I am to have my old school buddy here. Tonight the black depression that has been gnawing at me like a cancer is gone. I feel warm and pleasantly weary. Perhaps Wolff's presence will prove to be a good omen, I reflect sleepily. I close my eyes to the sound of Wolff's voice describing some school prank I had long since forgotten.

Next morning the news makes the rounds that Fur Cap is to be our camp commandant.

"He'll try to bury us soon enough," Wolff says laconically.

Around nine o'clock, although it is still dark, the guards distribute tools for the *lesozagotovka*, the wood-cutting operations. Notice is given in all the barracks that able-bodied adults, with the exception of mothers with children, are obliged to work in the forest. They are to receive a ration of 500 grams of bread per day, twenty grams of oil, and ten grams of sugar. Those who do not work are to receive 350 grams of bread per day. For the time being a nine-hour work day has been prescribed. Those failing to comply will go on piece-work. The instructions are short and clear.

We are to receive two daily meals from the Camp kitchen, which apparently is situated about two meters from the barracks compound. The kitchen is part of the Command Post, which includes the administrative offices, the guardhouse, and the commandant's residence.

By nine-thirty we are on our way to work. The supervisor, a husky young Red guard, leads us into the forest. We follow him in single file, as the snow lies a meter deep and more. I'm carrying a huge axe, the others carry mainly saws and hatchets.

Wolff has draped a red muffler around the collar of his short sheepskin. "It's a gesture of loyalty," he explains with his crooked half-grin. "Besides, the colors around here are pretty drab."

Ohm Peters is wearing a scuffed brown jacket, which is all he has left by way of short outer clothing. Neufeld lurches through the snow in felt boots several sizes too big. "You walk ahead," Koehn instructs him; "after you nobody'll get stuck."

Tielmann is wearing the serviceable leather jacket he purchased in Moscow; it cost him his last silver ruble at the time.

We reach the denser part of the forest now. Around us there is nothing but massive trees and between them seemingly bottomless snowdrifts. That's the entire geography of the North. I feel the depression settling in again. "How will we ever survive the appalling harshness, the sheer physical insensibility of this environment?" I ask myself. I stagger and almost knock down Wolff in front of me.

"You seem to be eager to get to work," he laughs. "Relax. The trees aren't going anywhere till we get there."

After a half-hour march we halt. The guard explains the blaze marks on the trees and we go to work. The deep forest silence gives way to the thunk of axes and the two-beat swish of the swede saws. Then, to the sounds of splintering trunks, the first pines come crashing down, showering masses of snow down on us from their crowns.

The hours go by. We work away silently and only occasionally look around to see where the others are and where the guard is lurking.

Wolff is the first to break the silence. "It's getting boring," he remarks. "Let's ration our energy—after all, everything else is rationed around here. Don't worry, we can tame the young fox who's guarding us. We'll take time to meditate and chat a bit. I want to tell you what I did after we graduated back in nineteen thirteen."

He swings lustily at his tree several times, then lets his hatchet stick in the wood.

"Do you know the Siberian city of Tomsk at all? Man, those were three interesting semesters I had at the Chemical Institute there. I studied some, of course, but my main interest was the boat trips we took along the Ob River—for a month or two at a time." His face softens in reflection.

The Fox has heard us talking and starts coming our way. Wolff spots him and says loudly, with a wink: "Winter expeditions in the North? I've given them up for the time being." He starts chopping vigorously again.

"Watch it!" Neufeld yells suddenly. The tree makes a whistling, rustling sound as it comes hurtling down in the spot hastily vacated by several other cutters.

The Fox has disappeared again. We resume our conversation as we start lopping the branches off the fallen tree.

"Well," continues Wolff, "then came the War, if you'll recall, and I found myself in the ambulance service on the Caucasian front. My unit was captured in nineteen sixteen—very routine, nothing heroic, believe me—and I served a sort of romantic Turkish imprisonment which gave me the chance to see Germany when the War was over. I wandered through Asia Minor by shank's mare and crossed the Balkans to Wuerttemberg. That's where my people came from originally.

"But revolution was in the air in Germany too. Somehow I couldn't persuade myself that a German revolution would be any more salubrious than a Russian one. Besides, you remember that I had elderly parents. So, I set off again—back this time, across the border and straight to Saratov." Dropping his jaunty tone he continues, "I don't have to tell you the rest. Since then everything has, as they say, gone more or less according to plan." His voice sinks still lower. "And this . . . " his mittened hand makes a downward motion, "is where the plan will be fulfilled, so to say."

We start swinging again. Was he a fool to have come back? A brave fool, perhaps. He must have known exactly what his fate would be. How like Wolff to do such a thing with a casualness that would strike others as foolhardy, perhaps even as sentimental nonsense. But his flippancy doesn't fool me. I know him too well.

By now our cutting area looks like a slaughter ground, with the trampled snow covered with severed branches and bright yellow woodchips from the butchered trees.

During a pause we hear a rough male voice singing in another cutting area not far away. The tune is the famous song about Stenka Razin,[1] but the words are different. The singing is punctuated by the regular beat of swinging hatchets:

> In Vologda's forests white—
> Hunger—graves—and icy night.
> Over Russia's northern jail
> Hear the blizzard's guilty wail.

Wolff is offended by the homemade doggerel. "Magnificent, this poetry," he mutters in distaste. "In addition to all the other abuses against one's senses—this one too." He grimaces again.

"You're ignoring the stirring tune," I come to the defense of the singer. "It recalls the heroic times of the celebrated robber chieftan of the Volga. Does the memory of Stenka Razin bother you? Why shouldn't his tragic story be updated and made relevant even to this setting?"

"You're right," Wolff smiles. "How could anyone in rags and on our miserable diet be expected to make better verses? Let us forgive the doggerel for the sake of the noble melody!"

"Over—Rus—sia's nor—thern ja—il . . . " the singer repeats with artless intensity.

At noon we make the half-hour march back to camp. Four of us from our barrack are sent to the camp kitchen with pails. Wolff and I, along with Koehn and Neufeld, go on this first trip. At the kitchen we make an interesting discovery: hundreds of Germans, Tartars, and Russians are standing in line there. It appears there are several more barrack compounds in the forest around the Command Post.

Queuing is taken for granted here. No one shows any impatience, even when it takes an hour to get served. After exactly fifty-five minutes we are back with the pails, which contain a thin broth with a few potatoes lying at the bottom. At least the stuff is still warm and we are hungry and cold. Penner makes a sly comment on the food by quoting from his beloved Fritz Reuter:

> Rindfleesh onn Plumen ess'n schoen't Gericht
> Doch, mine herrn, eck kriegt man nich.
> Roast beef with plums is nice to eat
> But, gentlemen, that's not my treat.

---

[1]Stenka Razin was a legendary peasant rebel of the seventeenth century who was finally captured and then beheaded in Red Square.

It's already getting dark when we march back to work. We try to follow our own footsteps, but from time to time we lose the track and fall behind the lead man. I estimate that we'll have four hours of grayish light daily and twenty hours of dusk or semi-darkness in this accursed place.

"What's more nourishing," Neufeld drawls sarcastically, "that kind of hot water or the crust of bread?"

"That's a problem too subtle for me to solve," Tielmann answers cynically.

We roll ourselves makhorka[2] cigarettes and start wielding our axes and saws again. The saws buzz until the tone rises to a whine; then everyone jumps out of the way and the tree comes thundering down.

The work warms us up; if only the fatigue weren't there.

Around eight in the evening we become aware of a light shining over the forest. "The north star!" Wolff exclaims. "Pretty soon it'll be able to shine down even on the Caucasus. We'll have this obstructing forest down in no time." We all enjoy a good laugh.

The trees stand so close together it is often difficult to free the felled trees from the branches of those still standing, especially the broad-shouldered pines. Occasionally the whole gang has to work on a felled tree before it can be dropped into the clearing.

We are pulling at a gnarled white pine. "One, two, three—down!" Neufeld gives the command. We let go and spring aside. The tree lands in the clearing with a resounding thud.

Where's old Peters? Didn't he hear the signal? We hear him groaning under the massive crown. We scrabble desperately to free him. Fortunately he is pinned under the lighter branches near the top and not under the trunk. Nevertheless he is pale and shaken and unable to rise to his feet unaided.

At the end of our first day in the forest we are dragging our first victim back to camp on a litter. Peters appears not to have suffered any broken bones but is badly bruised and very sore; he won't be doing any sawing for awhile.

The women and children who remain in the barracks are forced to get through the long dark afternoon and early evening without any light. The administration allows each family one liter of oil per month. This means we can light the lamps only for a brief period each evening. As much as possible we want to conserve our supplies of oil for the seventh day, the rest day which is prescribed by the regulations. We'll need the illumination then to carry out the essential tasks of patching, sewing, and washing—perhaps even letter-writing—which the work week leaves little time for and even less energy.

But we soon discover that the prescribed "rest day" is a false presumption on our part. Without a word of explanation the Commandant has simply cancelled rest days for the first few weeks.

Our work gang tries hard to get used to the arduous routine in the forest, and we suffer no further casualties. Only Ohm Peters remains behind on his

[2]*Makhorka* is a coarse, strong, home-grown tobacco.

bunk—a situation that he finds most disagreeable. For decades he had led the way on his farm in the village, and here too, even at his age, he was determined to set the example. In spite of his disappointment, however, he remains as uncomplaining and congenial as ever.

"Well, I guess we'll have to take our rest days in bits and pieces on the job," Wolff says with his usual cheerful irony. "After all, we owe it to the state to conserve our energy. We all know that Russia's gold mines are her forests. We still have huge,"—his long arms seem to encompass half the forest—"gigantic work norms to fulfill. So let's be mindful of our duty as citizens by not burning ourselves out regardless of what Fur Cap decrees."

After this we try to relax on the job as much as possible, always keeping a wary eye out for the Fox, of course. But we also realize that our tactic may result in a worsening of conditions for us, especially if our output goes down noticeably. The last thing we want to do is bring about even more stringent regulations which would affect all the prisoners. But the cruel irony is that the conditions are already so bad we don't have the strength to work a full nine-hour day even if we wanted to.

During the first week fatigue and anxiety about the future make it difficult for us to sleep at night. Alone in the dark each of us is tortured by the sure knowledge—a knowledge we do not speak about during the day—that we are fighting a losing battle here, that the odds are stacked overwhelmingly against us no matter how determined we are to survive. As carefully as we plan and brace ourselves for tomorrow, there will probably be one final tomorrow which we may not have the strength or resolution to face.

Our first rest day is finally announced for December first. Neufeld calls me over and confides his idea that this would be a good time to convert our small remaining sums of money into foodstuffs.

"Where?" I demand skeptically.

"We'll go to the nearest town, to Yenisseievka, where the post office is. I know how to get there."

"Look man, that's over twenty kilometers."

"I know, but we can't be sure we'll get another rest day before the end of the year."

Reluctantly, I concede the point. It will mean forfeiting the entire rest day. Wolff agrees to accompany us. At least the others will get their much-needed rest.

We start out very early, several hours before dawn. We don't want our departure to be noticed, if possible. The route to town has been carefully described to us by people at the Camp kitchen.

The stars are shimmering over the forest. The only sound is the crunching of snow underfoot. Each of us has an old gunny sack slung over his shoulder. I have carefully added up all the money the others have entrusted to me and we have decided in advance exactly what we are going to purchase. If we find we can't carry everything, we'll have to hire a peasant with a horse to take us back to camp.

Yenisseievka is a fair-sized village with well over a hundred huts, a small post office, a state store, and a ruined church.

"It's contemporary Russia in miniature," Wolff quips as we enter the village.

"In that case we probably won't find any food to buy from the peasants either," Neufeld adds drily.

The single long street is silent and empty. We stop and survey the double row of houses, undecided what we should do next. Then a tiny peasant in a huge cap comes hobbling along. Wolff boldly opens the bargaining.

"Good morning, Uncle! Do you need any silver?"

The old man knows the score. He looks us over carefully while scratching under his greasy cap with grubby fingers.

Khorosho, okay, come along," he mutters and looks around cautiously.

In the peasant's frugally heated room Wolff opens our purse.

"All right, here's a fiver, old man. Have you got flour?"

"I've got flour—of course, I've got flour. Fourteen kilograms."

"Eighteen."

"That's a lot."

"The silver is more."

"Sixteen."

"Eighteen."

The old man examines the silver coin carefully and lets it ring on the table. *Khorosho*—eighteen," he says after a bit more reflection and disappears into his storeroom.

It's as quiet in the hut as outside on the street. Wolff stands by the window drumming his fingers nervously. It's broad daylight now. The straw-thatched roofs are thin and inferior-looking and indicate the poverty of the inhabitants. These semi-farmers have to support themselves in winter either by woodcutting or by hunting and trapping for furs which they sell in Archangel or Vologda.

"Look out, men," Wolff calls out softly. A Red Guard, carbine slung over his shoulder, is crossing the street in our direction. Keeping our eyes on the window we move quickly to the door, but apparently the soldier hasn't seen us. He disappears behind the adjoining house and we breathe again.

The peasant returns with a suspension scale and methodically weighs off the flour in five-kilogram lots under our watchful eyes.

Our first transaction concluded, we leave the sack with the peasant and move on. A few houses farther down the street we obtain some buckwheat. Then we rest for awhile and eat the bit of bread we have brought. A little later we try another hut, where the friendly, rotund housewife not only agrees to sell us some fresh horse meat but invites us to sit down for a cup of hot tea. It's only five kilograms of meat, but it's a welcome find. We chat with the woman and then take our leave.

"I suppose a person can get used to anything—even horse meat," Neufeld growls.

"My dear man," Wolff flashes his grin, "we are voluntary resettlers, pioneers especially chosen by the state not only for our unique working skills, but also for our well-known ability to adapt quickly and efficiently to new conditions and circumstances."

Neufeld mutters something unintelligible.

About two-thirty it is already getting dusk as we collect our various purchases. They weigh between fifty-five and sixty kilograms. After deliberating about how to transport our burden, we decide to return on foot.

The return journey proves to be more difficult than we expected. We have divided the contents of the sacks equally, but Neufeld has plainly overtaxed himself and staggers like a drunk under his load. Wolff and I slow our pace as much as possible.

In spite of his fatigue, Neufeld becomes talkative when we sit down to rest. He has something on his mind.

"What do you think, Wolff? Do people in Germany know what's happening to us here?" he blurts out.

Wolff and I exchange glances. "And here I thought you were about done in," Wolff jokes. "Where do you get the energy for such bright ideas?"

Suddenly he is serious. "You're right to ask the question, of course. It's sad to see how we've lost contact with the old country. What do they know about us by now? A few moldy, out-of-date statistics, perhaps. A few experts interested for scholarly reasons may have a bit more knowledge about the ethnic Germans and Mennonites in this country. But that's about all.

"I can tell you that during my two years over there I was usually referred to as a 'German Russian', a sort of half-breed freak—which to some people meant that I was a German on the way to becoming a Russian and to others a Russian quaintly trying to be a German. But enough of that." He waves his hand. "If you're asking me whether the Germans, or the rest of the world as far as that goes, know about his whole ungodly mess, the answer is no, my friend! How could they possibly? Through a few topical items in their provincial newspapers?'

We get up and start walking again. I am struck by a new idea. "You know, we could bring our plight to the attention of the people over there by writing to them ourselves, by bombarding them with letters. That would make them sit up and notice."

There is silence as the other two ponder my suggestion. Sleeves rubbing against jackets make a whistling sound as we trudge along with our heavy sacks. Neufeld stops to hitch up his sack, which continually threatens to slide off his shoulder.

He stands there looking at me expectantly. "Do you have any direct contacts in Germany?"

"Well yeah, sort of, I guess—distant relatives on my mother's side." I turn to Wolff. "But you must have more recent connections, Wolff—right?"

He is not exactly encouraging. "It might be worth a try. All it takes is a scrap of Soviet paper, a stamp—and the risk. But you know that in this country the sound of bells does not carry very far."

We walk on silently, lost in thought. Judging by the stars it must be close to nine o'clock. After a brief spell we see the glimmer of lights in the Command Post.

We find our barrack in an uproar. Apparently Ohm Peters had invited all those interested to attend a church service in our Barrack Number Seven at eleven in the morning. The barrack had been full to overflowing. Even Father Nikolai, accompanied by several other Russians, had attended.

The service no sooner began with the singing of a chorale when a guard appeared and demanded to know who had convened the "meeting." There was a strained silence. Then Peters stepped forward and tried to give an explanation. But the fellow refused to listen and bluntly ordered the old man to follow him.

At the Command Post he was subjected to a lengthy interrogation.

"What were you trying to accomplish with this meeting, you old serpent?" The Commandant was crude as always.

Peters told the truth. "To hold a church service, Citizen Commandant."

"So. You are laboring under a gigantic illusion, citizen. You are here to discharge your obligations to the State. Do you understand that?" He regarded Peters sarcastically. "God? You'd be a lot better off here if you'd left your God behind on the Volga—ha-ha!"

But Ohm Peters stood his ground. "Citizen Commandant, without God, we can't exist. No one . . . .."

"—Shut your yap!" roared Fur Cap, suddenly livid. "You want slavery, you old shit? All right, fine. You're on report!"

The innocent old man was put on report. The interrogation ended with a sentence of detention for eight days.

The special cells are located near the camp kitchen, so it was possible at least to slip the old man's coat to him. The pockets of the coat had been quickly filled with rusks in the event that his rations would be reduced.

Now we know where the boundary line of our existence is when it comes to holding religious services. We are to be deprived even of that consolation.

We have worked out a system for supplementing our meagre rations. While the guards are keeping an eye on us in the forest, the women roast some of the bartered flour. For dinner at noon they thicken our watery soup with the browned flour; in this way we can all enjoy a more nourishing diet. Thus, our main meal is almost bearable and it gives us the strength to face the long, dark afternoon among the pines.

Looking toward the future we dread, more than anything, the time when our driblets of cash will have melted away. As long as most of us are still able to work we are at least assured of our basic daily rations; however, they are not enough to satisfy our hunger. Our strength is gradually waning. We recall sadly that in spite of the hardships, life on the collective was much more bearable.

For several days Tielmann has been wrapping a double strip of cotton around his throat. He has developed sores which bother him badly on the job. He never complains, but I notice on our weekly visits to the bathhouse that the sores are spreading over his entire body.

How I loathe that camp bathhouse! The small sauna room is always impossibly crowded with up to forty men, so that we are forced into frequent contact with each other. We are painfully aware of the sick people of all kinds who come here, and we try as much as we can to avoid direct contact with ulcerous and rash-covered bodies. We squat in front of the glowing fieldstones and try to sweat as much as possible. But the sweating enervates our already enfeebled bodies to the point where some of us are forced to sit in the changing room for an hour or so before we are ready to undertake the walk back to the barracks.

Young Willie Koehn is the first to become infected. One evening he shows his father his badly scratched fingers. The rash between his fingers bothers him so much that he lies awake at night moaning. At work he wears his mother's last pair of cloth gloves. He comes to work with us for a few more days, but is constantly losing his gloves and complaining about his itch. The risk of the rest of us being infected makes us decide to leave him home for awhile.

Ohm Peters has been released from detention and now spends much of his time in his bunk. In the evening we usually find him sitting in front of the open stove door reading his Bible. His face is growing more pallid and sombre every day. But his debilitated condition has not affected his patriarchal role among us. He is as ready as ever to give counsel and solace to those of us on the edge of despair. Thank God there are human powers which remain intact even when the body is impaired.

"It's when we are most in need that we see the clearest proof of God's love," he likes to say. "So, our need is also our salvation," he concludes with a sweet simplicity that is irresistible.

In normal circumstances one might find such a faith a little naive and sentimental. But ours are not normal circumstances. The brutally elemental world to which we have been condemned demands an equally elemental faith. We already know that whatever hope for survival we have depends not only on keeping our bodies alive but our souls also. The most insidious enemy in camp life is the kind of spreading indifference which begins as callousness towards fellow sufferers and ends as a general apathy so pervasive one's very soul is frozen into it. Indifference to one's own fate is the camp disease from which no one recovers.

Even Wolff drops his ironic manner in Ohm Peters' presence.

"Friends," the old man begins one evening in his amiable way, "Christmas is coming; in ten days the Christian world will be celebrating. We must try to get permission from the Commandant—"

"—to rest up and try to forget for a bit," Neufeld breaks in viciously. His bitterness at times threatens to get out of hand.

"That too," the old man goes on unperturbed. "But I fear our souls are beginning to wither along with our bodies here. We need something more than physical rest to revive us."

Tielmann is positive. "I agree, we'll hold a celebration."

"With a Christmas tree," Mrs. Koehn puts in hopefully.

The subject immediately attracts the attention of the children. The women sitting on the various bunks look up from their small tasks. "Christmas," murmurs the little Albrecht lad dreamily.

Wolff's voice carries almost as much weight as Ohm Peters. "There'll be no nonsense," he says firmly. "Definitely a tree, and the Christmas story, Ohm Jasch, and songs—who knows, perhaps even gifts?"

By now we are all caught up by the exciting prospect of actually celebrating Christmas in our bleak barrack. As if by magic, Ohm Peters has managed to bind us together in a group undertaking that will rehumanize us and lift us for a moment out of this filthy existence.

A week before Christmas a widow and her two grown daughters are assigned to our barrack. They are a Mennonite family from the Crimea. Mrs. Preuss is a quiet, frail-looking woman with a mournful face. The daughters, Martha and Theresa, are handsome, vivacious young women who show signs of breeding and sophistication, although their faces betray the cruel marks of prolonged deprivation that we know only too well. They are clearly not country girls; their confident air and assured manner smack of the city or town.

The girls tell us that the three of them had been earmarked for the North a year ago because their mother, made desperate by hunger, had taken a few ears of corn from a harvest wagon on the collective. The act constituted theft of state property, the manager had solemnly explained to them. Such despairing acts of theft were regular occurrences on their collective and were always punished with banishment, or worse. The sentences were pronounced in a completely routine manner, devoid of either malice or pity. Sending people into exile was a purely administrative matter which involved no more than a little paper work for the officials who were responsible.

For the first few days the new prisoners try to rest up from their long journey. By way of food they have brought only a small sack of dried fruit and a little maize. We offer them some of our own fare, but it is obvious that one or more of them will have to come out to work if they are to eke out a subsistence here. By the fourth day, Martha, the twenty-one-year-old older daughter, has decided to go into the forest with us.

We assign her the job of pruning the smaller branches of the felled trees. "That's the kind of tidying-up job consistent with feminine nature and training," Wolff observes in his usual dry manner.

But he is surprisingly solicitous. He shows Martha Preuss exactly what to do and hovers around her in a way that is almost comical. That he is drawn to our new work companion is as obvious as it is surprising. I happen to know that it is no accident that Wolff never got married. Even during our adolescence he was known as a man's man who neither desired nor sought much female companionship. Perhaps he has always had a deep-seated fear of any emotional entanglement. Under that ironical manner there must be a deeply passionate man who has never come to terms with himself. I can only guess. For all his witty, sympathetic interest in others, Wolff is curiously reticent when it comes to discussing his own private life.

Martha Preuss's Russian is flawless. I note that when she converses with Father Nikolai. She must have gone to a Russian high school. The priest is as charmed by her as the rest of us are. At work she wears a brown woollen man's cap over her clean, tidy hair. She has a pretty face which in repose is slightly marred by two deep folds running from her eyes to the corners of her mouth. More eloquently than any words could, they reveal the kind of life she has been forced to lead.

Martha tells us at work that her father started as a village preacher in the Crimea. He became so popular that he was called to serve as an evangelical preacher in Simferopol, where the girls grew up. Her father courageously kept on preaching even after the May, 1928 edict against religion was made known. Shortly thereafter he was arrested and sentenced to ten years at Lake Baykal in Siberia. He died there eight months later. After her father's arrest the family moved back to their native village, which was now part of a collective.

Martha speaks about her family's fate calmly and matter-of-factly. But there is a resonance in her tone when she describes her father's sad end which betrays the depths of her feelings. Wolff listens to her intently and observes every nuance of her changing expressions.

The two are rapidly becoming close friends. They converse freely at the work site and Wolff does little favors for the girl whenever he can. His comments are still tart, but flavored by a more amiable manner, a manner made up of a kind of gruff, old-fashioned gallantry that is almost ludicrously at variance with Wolff's independence of character and our generally miserable conditions here.

"Are you fond of our Russian literature?" he asks Martha at work one day.

"Of course, above all our romantic writers."

Wolff is delicately condescending. "Like Zhukovsky?[3] *The Twelve Sleeping Maidens?*" He obviously considers that to be the kind of light reading a romantically inclined young lady would prefer.

Martha laughs, perfectly aware of Wolff's patronizing implication. Yes, that too. But even more the young Pushkin."

"For example?" he pursues, a little surprised.

"The Robber Brothers."[4]

Wolff looks sheepish. By naming Pushkin's long, Byronic narrative poem set in the Crimea she shows that there is nothing naive or school-girlish in her literary tastes. She has gently put Wolff in his place and he knows it.

Just before Christmas the Commandant goes on a trip. It's a stroke of luck; we'll be able to celebrate Christmas without interference. But on the morning of the twenty-fourth the deputy commander, a surly Cossack who is himself

---

[3]V. A. Zhukovsky (1783-1852), poet and translator, was an important percursor of Pushkin in helping to shape Russian verse style and form. He specialized in light Romantic landscape poems and folk ballads.

[4]*Bratya razboiniki, The Robber Brothers* (1827) is one of Pushkin's (1799-1837) masterpieces. The poem describes the dramatic escape from prison of two brothers who, although chained and fettered, were able to swim across the Dnieper to freedom.

serving a sentence here, informs us that we'll have to work the full day. After that he doesn't care what we do.

"Well, it looks like another forest celebration," Tielmann says philosophically.

Our mood is more doleful than usual as we trudge to work. We feel depressed and defeated. Only Neufeld whistles to himself, in a way that is irritating to the rest of us, as though he knew that our hopes for a holiday had been futile.

To add to our misery, it's a bitterly cold day. My thermometer registered minus thirty-seven when we left the barrack. The cold makes it impossible for us to take the long conversation breaks we had planned. We have to keep working to keep from freezing. Koehn, wielding a huge red handkerchief, is the first to wipe the sweat from his brow.

"There's another Christmas miracle for you—to be able to sweat in this cold," Neufeld sneers.

No one laughs. A few of us try to strike up a conversation, but the spark is missing. The extreme cold and our gloomy thoughts combine to keep us apart. Our usual group intimacy is gone. Even Wolff seems to be sulking today. Perhaps because Martha Preuss is holding herself aloof from him, and from the rest of us. Without pausing, she works steadily, head bent, with prim concentration. I peel my trunk down to where she is standing and see that her eyes are red. Poor thing! Wolff appears not to notice, but perhaps he is avoiding her because he does not want to intrude on her private grief.

In this way the day plods along into darkness, and our disappointment gradually subsides as weariness takes over.

Bone-weary and despondent, we return at night to find a small Christmas tree set up in the barrack. An oil lamp has been carefully suspended over its slender tip. The branches are draped with shimmering threads of tinfoil. There is a festive air in the place, with everyone wearing his improvised Sunday best. The women look pale but happy in their cheap black dresses. The children are standing or kneeling entranced before a half-open chest standing beside the tree. The chest bears the name and address of Ohm Peters, printed in large, black letters across its top. There are a few guests from Barrack Number Eight next door, including Bergen, his wife, and their infant son. Mrs. Bergen looks tired and wan as she breast-feeds her baby.

From his place before the roaring stove, Ohm Peters, ruddy-faced, chants greetings to us as we come in. He looks very pleased with himself. "When you're ready, we'll all assemble," he cries. He reminds me suddenly of my childhood when my father would ceremoniously summon us children to gather for such special events as Christmas and Easter.

There is a flurry of activity as we hastily wash and change out of our grimy, sodden work clothes. Wolff dons his much-patched old student uniform which is too large for him now, and sits down soberly at the foot of his bunk. Koehn and I are wearing linen blouses—our last legacy of former prosperity—under our faded jackets. I glance down at the crude wooden *schlorre* on my feet and think fondly of the soft leather slippers I once purchased in Saratov and wore in the house for years.

Ohm Peters leads the singing in his reedy, breathy voice. "Silent night, holy night," he begins. We all join in, a little hesitant and self-conscious at first. It's a long time since we've sung together ceremoniously like this. Then Wolff's magnificent basso rolls through the barrack like a force of nature, confident and irresistible. He sweeps us along. For a moment our voices surge as one, then peel off into the familiar parts.

Sleep in heavenly peace,
Sleep in heavenly peace.

We look at each other as though making new discoveries about ourselves.

With the second stanza our singing begins to ebb. The women are sobbing openly and one after the other is forced to break off. Koehn manfully takes over the melody line but his singing has more robustness than beauty in it. With Wolff's voice more dominant than ever, we conclude the last stanza with a mere half dozen voices. Then there is a hush as we sit and wait, the women weeping gently, the men and children subdued and respectful.

Ohm Peters starts reading the story of the Nativity according to St. Luke. His voice is halting and tremulous. I fear that the old man will lose control and spoil the majesty of the hour. But he paces himself carefully, with long pauses between verses, and manages to get through to the end.

Again a deepening silence. We know that we have reached the last frontier of human speech. Spontaneously, as one, we all slip over into personal meditation, into a form of inner communication too profound for words . . ..
So the minutes pass . . ..

The bits of tinfoil are beginning to rustle from the heat. The children are squirming and sighing with impatience.

Ohm Peters says a closing prayer, then gets up ponderously and points to the chest. "Now then, they've sent along my last possessions. Let's see what we've got here." He raises the lid all the way and takes out a muffler.

"Here, Teacher, that's for you—you need something for that sore throat of yours." He tosses the muffler over to Tielmann, who accepts it gratefully.

"This is a New Testament," the old man says in his stilted Russian. "Father Nikolai, may you rejoice in it on this day and many days hereafter." He hands the book to the priest, who bows, crosses himself and then, unable to contain his joy, embraces Ohm Peters and kisses him on both cheeks.

It is almost as if Ohm Peters had ordered the chest especially for the occasion. There seems to be some small, appropriate gift for everybody. The children receive a few homemade syrup bonbons which they suck ecstatically.

Although we are grateful for Ohm Peters' gifts, we are a little embarrassed that the gift-giving is so one-sided.

"Ohm Jasch, will you accept this cap—?" But he declines firmly. "I require nothing more than I already have."

The women now tend to the tea-making, relieved to be doing something again after giving vent to their emotions. They look more animated than they have since leaving home. Our festive tea-drinking is accompanied by lively conversation. Father Nikolai gives us men a vivid account of Christmas celebrations in the Orthodox Church. Then Wolff, in his inimitable style, describes how a typical German family observes Christmas. We are all in an expansive mood and the talk goes on and on.

Theresa Preuss is the center of attention in the women's circle as she recalls Christmas experiences from the past, including a charming account of a sleigh ride through the snowy steppe at night when they were spending Christmas with her mother's family in the Molochnaja one year. The ride was made even more exciting by a hilarious minor mishap when the sleigh overturned and everybody was tumbled screaming into the snow. The girl is a masterful storyteller and imparts to her simple story all the enchantment and romantic nostalgia of a fairy tale. Then, in a more serious vein, she relates how she and Martha accompanied their father one Christmas as he distributed some desperately needed food packages in a slum district in Simferopol. She sighs deeply and adds: "If only we had some of those packages now . . .." Mrs. Preuss begins to weep quietly during this account and Theresa embraces her afterwards and is tenderly attentive to her mother.

Yet there is something about Theresa Preuss that makes me uneasy. A pretty girl of nineteen, she looks strong and healthy; but she has made no move to join her sister in the forest work, even though that means the three women have to subsist on only one full ration and two part-rations. Her elaborate pretense of looking after her fragile mother does not fool me, and I know from Wolff that it does not fool Martha either. Theresa's selfishness is out of place here. For all her vivacious charm there is an insensitivity about her which I find disturbing.

Martha has joined Wolff and they are sitting somewhat apart. They are deep in conversation and oblivious to the general hub-bub. As usual, they seem to be conversing in Russian. I roll myself a last *makhorka* cigarette and reflect on the increasing differences I detect between the Preuss sisters.

It's after midnight when we retire to our bunks; tomorrow is a workday.

On New Year's Eve Barrack Number Seven gets another surprise. The student, Heinrich Sudermann, has suddenly turned up. He is even shabbier looking than he was before his disappearance in Moscow. His face is incredibly pale and bewildered-looking. We try asking him questions but his answers are cryptic and incoherent.

"What's to say?" He can't meet our glances. "Blood-betrayal, death. What else? Education, part of education, you know." His ashen face twists into a grimace and he snickers noisily.

"Where were you when we left Moscow, Sudermann?"

"Ha-ha-ha, visiting the Cheka. Yes, nice quiet chat . . . friends, news, catching up . . . ha-heh-heeeeee . . .." His laugh shrills to a maniacal pitch.

"No more questions," Wolff's voice cuts through the boy's wild cackle. "They've sucked him dry and sent us the husk, the vampires."

Next morning Sudermann accompanies us to the forest, but he is taciturn and withdrawn. Whenever he pauses in his work he looks up at the trees and sky and shakes his head. It is as though his poor demented mind cannot reconcile this vast, majestic, impersonal forest world with the cruelly perverted little prison world which has broken his spirit and then casually spit out his body to rot.

Another curtly worded regulation reaches us. From now on "the school-aged children of voluntary resettlers will receive food rations only if they attend the nursery school." The regulation fools no one. It's another step in the process of "bolshevization," and a shrewd one. What can the parents do when failure to comply means a further diminution of their already scanty bread ration? With heavy hearts the Koehns and Mrs. Albrecht are forced to expose their little ones to the crass propagandizing of a Soviet school. Even Penner allows his retarded lad to attend. "There's not much they can do to him—except feed him," he reasons.

The first few evenings the children are eager to report their activities in school. They are glad to be released from the monotony of the barrack and are no longer bored and listless. Already they can sing the popular Red Army marching song "Budenny's Cavalry." They know all the stanzas of the "Internationale", and Koehn's five-year-old lad proudly warbles the Communist funeral march "Innocent Victims."

The parents are indignant but helpless. "There's nothing we can do about it," Koehn says morosely. "Our children are growing up in two different worlds."

"There'll only be one world in the end, Koehn," is Neufeld's cynical rejoinder.

The remark is uncalled for. Neufeld's family grew up long ago during the good times, but even then it did not turn out well. His oldest son was killed while serving with the Whites in the Civil War. His two younger sons were unable to get along with their autocratic and cantankerous father and ran away to Saratov to work in a factory. One of his daughters eloped with a Russian grain buyer from Kazan, and the other was a mousy thing who finally found a Mennonite husband in remote Orenburg. Deserted by all his children long before his arrest, Neufeld now has only his aging wife, who is almost as unlikeable as he is. And then to end up here. Small wonder he is so embittered, and getting worse every day. I pity the man, I suppose we all do, but he is hard to take at times.

In mid-January Wolff finally writes to his acquaintances in Worms. After squeezing my brains trying to remember the address of my relatives, I also write my first letter to Germany. We write during moments when we are not being observed. Our fear is that the letters will not get out of the country or if they do that they will not elicit a response. If that happens this last hope will be dashed for the others too.

On January twenty-fourth we finally get another rest-day. As it happens, Penner is preparing to go to Yenisseievka. We give him our letters to mail. I give him the money for postage and caution him to be careful and discreet.

"Smoke doesn't necessarily mean a fire," Wolff says wryly after Penner has left. "In the final analysis the censor can't blame us for sending a greeting to relatives in another country."

"We're writing for better reasons than sending greetings, my friend," I counter. "Assuming that the censor is the idiot you imply he is, it'll take two or three weeks for the letters to get there. Again, assuming that they bother to answer at all, we should be hearing from them in about five to six weeks."

"Neatly reckoned, old pal. You still know how to dream, Alexander! But you forget that it is a real world out there. Tell me something Sasha. Why are we trying so hard to prolong our miserable existence here anyway?" His fingers tighten on my shoulder. "Listen, friend, we'll be gnawing our little piece of bitter bread here till the end. You know that! Stop dreaming—tomorrow's another workday."

He's right, of course. For us tomorrow is just another workday—a line of workdays running straight ahead to the vanishing point like railway tracks to the horizon.

At the beginning of February I become the first person in the barrack to receive a letter from home. It is from my brother-in-law Peter Enns, who was lucky enough to be away on a business trip when the arrests were made. I read it eagerly in the privacy of my bunk, but the others besiege me to the point where I am obliged to read it aloud.

Mariental,
January 22.

Dear A. This is not the first answer to your card of November 29 which I have sent. One has to assume that on both sides letters are going astray. So I'll repeat some items. First, on the day before Christmas Eve we were visited at night by people who are apparently carrying out systematic raids on our colony. They took the last of our better clothing and the best of our food supplies, so we could celebrate a "lighter Christmas" as they put it.

The population is bitter and unruly in the aftermath of the very mediocre harvest. In the Tatar villages the shortage of bread is catastrophic. There are stories of cannibalism. I refused to believe them at first, but they have now been reliably confirmed—I won't say anymore about that! On a trip to Tsaritsyn[5] recently I saw a group of displaced peasants on the Volga shore scraping the hair off raw leather and cooking soup with it.

Conditions are not all that much better in our colony. The collective has to get by on rationed and ersatz provisions. There is a terrible shortage of fuel—even the supplies of dried dung are gone because collectivization has as good as destroyed the cattle herds. As if that isn't bad enough, we are experiencing an unusually severe winter.

Ernestine is spinning night and day so that we can trade wool for foodstuffs.

I know there isn't much consolation for you in all this. We think of you daily and of how we can in some way help you. If it's any consolation, you have left behind nothing to be regretted—except our love. When

[5]Tsaritsyn was a city on the South Volga which later became famous as Stalingrad and is now called Volgograd.

everything is said and done we are all trapped in the same leaky boat.
Ernestine and the children send their love and greetings.
Try to bear up, old man, and write again.

With love, P.

Somebody coughs softly in the silence. "So it's no warmer in the South than
here in the North," Neufeld rasps. He scowls down the row at Tielmann,
Wolff, and me. "So much for your fine theories and educated talk about the
changing system improving conditions and about public indignation. We're
stuck here and they're stuck there. And that's that!"

"That's the principle of equality at work, Neufeld," Wolff retorts. "You can
see the steady progress of Communism in that letter. Even the elements are
co-operating with the noble experiment. And you have the nerve to voice your
personal prejudices by criticizing an inevitable process?"

Neufeld gives Wolff another ferocious look but has nothing more to say.

Young Sudermann works quietly and uncomplainingly alongside the rest of
us, but he remains distant and we leave him alone. He has suffered enough.

One day, however, he enacts a terrifying scene in the forest. He is standing
at the edge of the clearing looking up at the sky as usual when suddenly
something in him snaps. With a hair-raising shriek he leaps up on a large,
felled trunk and delivers a loud speech accompanied by histrionic arm-
waving. The speech is in Russian! If only his outburst had been in German, so
that the guard hadn't understood it.

With chilling precision the poor wretch describes the interior of the Cheka
building in Moscow. He is mimicking the voice of a Cheka official.

"Those, gentlemen, are the cells: five by seven meters—not too small, so
that every prisoner can be secretly watched by suffering comrades . . . . We
leave the ground floor and descend to the basement. Here we see the torture
room—lined with rubber, of course, the doors doubly padded. Permit me to
present an actual case—that of the student Sudermann, a man of suspicious
connections. You can see for yourselves how we have managed to harness this
unruly character and make him docile. We've brought him around to a proper
understanding of things—aaargh, uh . . . .."

He gags at this point, makes some weird guttural noises, finally catches his
breath, and sails on. "You understand, gentlemen, that we must be prepared
to sacrifice everything to the idea of freedom. Sacrifice is the very life-blood
of our new Soviet state. We are building for the future, for a state in which
everyone will enjoy freedom. Those who deny freedom must be taught to
accept it. Yes, freedom means sacrifice, one hundred and fifty million people
must be ready to sacrifice for the sake of our glorious dream of free . . . .."

Transfixed by the boy's demented outburst, we see too late that the Fox has
come up behind him. The rifle butt crashes against his back and sends him
hurtling head first into the snow.

When we arrive at camp that evening Sudermann is taken directly to the Command Post. He does not return.

One morning Ohm Peters's health takes a sudden turn for the worse. He is trembling all over and looks flushed and sweaty. I ask him if there is anything I can do for him. "Just you go to work," he says with an effort. "It's probably just a touch of flu; I'll be all right by evening."

It looks more like a touch of malaria to me.

By evening the old man has lost consciousness. Tossing and raving, he preaches incoherent sermons and recalls bits and pieces of our long journey up here. Then, over and over, he recites the names of his fellow-sufferers. He is seriously ill.

We decide to notify the Commandant. For once the Commandant is in an obliging mood and places a sleigh at our disposal. He orders two of us to take Peters to the hospital in Andreievka and provides us with the necessary papers.

I decide to take Tielmann along so he can have the doctor look at his festering sores.

It is only twenty-eight kilometers to the hospital, but it seems much longer. Our rawboned horse makes no attempt to set a brisk pace. To make things worse, as soon as we leave the protection of the forest we find ourselves facing a blinding snowstorm, a typical northern *buran*. It howls and swirls over the fields and repeatedly brings the nag to a helpless standstill. Eyes squeezed shut, fur collars pulled up, we try to place our bodies in positions to protect the sick man as much as possible from the icy blasts.

"Rather different this, from Pushkin's pretty snow poems," Tielmann gasps.

Like an invading army, wind and snow infiltrate every crevice and exposed part of our bodies, so that soon we are chilled to the marrow in spite of our thick wrappings.

The horse is standing again, quivering. The gale rocks it from side to side whipping its spindly shanks. Within minutes the snow begins to build up in front of the sleigh. Will we finally get snowed under completely? All we can do is sit and wait as the snow piles up.

"Only the wolves are missing now to complete the romantic scene," I shout against the wind.

Tielmann has had enough. He mutters something and heaves himself out of the sleigh. He grabs the bridle and with loud shouts leads the cowed animal out of the snowdrift. We take turns repeating this procedure every few minutes, but we can only guess at our direction. At least we are moving again, which is less terrifying than sitting still and freezing.

Gradually the *buran* begins to subside and we are relieved to find that we have not strayed far off course. We can again see the roadmarks indicating the sides of the road although some of these markers—tufts of straw tied to willow stakes set in the snow—have been knocked down by the blizzard.

In Andreievka we have to wait a long time before Ohm Peters is called in for his examination. The examination also takes considerable time. The military doctor, a not unfriendly man, diagnosis malaria, as I had suspected. "We'll keep him here for àwhile," he says finally. Then, with eyes averted, he quietly adds: "He requires a better diet to get well."

The doctor looks at Tielmann's ulcers, shakes his head, and gives him some ointment.

Father Nikolai is getting homesick for his own kind. Although he is in our company daily and we try to oblige him by conversing mainly in Russian, he yearns for his own people; he wants to serve his own congregation again. He is a shepherd without a flock and feels deprived and unused. His passionate nature demands to be fulfilled in pastoral work and priestly duties.

"It is precisely in a situation such as this that a congregation is most essential," he explains to Wolff and me. "Otherwise we'll all topple individually, like the trees we cut. The true faith can exist only within the Church."

On the last day of March he disappears. "He must have lost his appetite for all this," Neufeld observes in his usual acid manner. There is a look in Neufeld's eyes these days I do not like.

The priest is gone for six days. Fortunately we are able to cover up for him during his absence and there are no repercussions when he returns. He looks worn-out and sick, but his face is radiant as he tells Wolff and me what he has been doing.

"I've been searching for a flock," he sighs blissfully, "and God be praised I've found them . . ." He pauses, and a shadow passes over his pale features. "There are so many of them, so many new settlements are springing up all around us in the forest. There are literally thousands of my people sharing our fate here."

"And what now, Father?" Wolff inquires.

"Now I invite you both, my sons, to join our Easter celebration in the forest." He nods his shaggy head rapidly, as he always does when he is excited. "Yes, we are going to celebrate an Easter mass—at night, it'll have to be at night, of course. But that's the right time for it, the right time exactly." He chuckles contentedly, then grows thoughtful. "Yes, the right time for us believers in exile to celebrate is at night. Yes, that's very fitting."

Wolff receives his first letter from Germany. He is strangely secretive about it, and I guess that the news is not encouraging. But I make no inquiries; I know he will tell me when he is ready.

After brooding about it for a few days, he talks to me about it. "If you receive the same kind of answer, old man, I'd suggest we both stop pestering the illustrious citizens of that highly civilized country out there. They're not really concerned about a few northern pioneers like us . . .." He gives me a mournful look. "Sasha, we German Mennonites chose to live in isolated colonies in this country for almost a century and a half. Now we must be prepared to die in isolation too. After all, that's only logical, isn't it?"

"You sound almost as bitter as Neufeld," I say as he hands me the letter.

It is neatly written in a proper formal style. I run my eyes over the smooth, stereotyped phrases: The pleasure of hearing from you again, even though your circumstances leave much to be desired . . . . But, as a result of the current economic conditions, the writer's own circumstances are such as to make it difficult if not impossible to show his sympathy to the degree he would wish to do . . . . However, he will try to take the appropriate steps to provide whatever assistance he can . . . . In the meantime, with best wishes he remains, etc.

I hand the letter back to Wolff without comment. That night I sleep badly.

Next morning, on the way to work, I say to Wolff, "Listen, all those polite phrases—they don't add up to much, do they?"

"They add up to a great deal, friend," he answers curtly. "They inform us politely that we can now think of ourselves as exiles in a double sense."

In early April we get our first thaw, although there are still precious few signs of spring. In the Russian North, according to Wolff, even spring doesn't dare make a direct appearance; she has to send out a few advance scouts who can tell her whether to advance or retreat. "In any case, it's a pretty brief occupation." He shows his lop-sided grin for the first time since receiving the letter.

The thaw creates footwear problems for us. Our felt boots are no longer serviceable. Those who brought along leather boots wear them whenever they leave the barrack. The patches of ice between the mounds of moss slowly melt during the brief daylight hours and turn into dangerous sloughs which go down to a depth of several meters. Only the forest trees stand on solid ground.

The nocturnal frosts continue, but they are less severe now. One morning at work a graceful flight of swans passes so high overhead we can barely hear their calls. We put down our tools and gaze after them until they disappear over the tree tops.

"They prefer the south too, Vladimir Ivanovitch," Martha Preuss says wistfully to Wolff.

"Yeah, Marfa Petrovna, along with Neufeld they must be about the last individualists left in Russia."

The Russian Easter is drawing near. Father Nikolai has promised to keep me informed so that I can participate in the ceremony. On April fourteenth he draws me aside. "It's on for tonight," he whispers conspiratorially. "We'll go together."

Wolff and Tielmann, who had earlier expressed interest, have changed their minds about going. Wolff decides reluctantly that he can't afford to miss a whole night's sleep, and Tielmann simply does not feel up to the long walk.

That evening Father Nikolai and I get ready to go. I oil my boots one more time and he takes out the black robe, the silver cross, and the censer which he has carefully preserved with his few other belongings.

It's a fine clear night. The priest knows the route but we have to pick our way slowly and cautiously to avoid the deep puddles on all sides. Once he slips and I manage to grab his arm just as he begins to teeter over the murky waters. He is such a vital man it is easy to forget that he is well into middle age. The walk tires him but he refuses to stop for a rest.

It takes us almost three hours to walk the eight kilometers along the edge of the forest. Suddenly Father Nikolai stops and peers intently into the forest. Through the trees we catch a faint glimmer of lights and the sound of voices. "There they are," the priest murmurs happily.

A crowd of several hundred peasants has gathered in a huge natural clearing. They are all holding lighted wax candles. More people keep arriving from all directions, also bearing candles. The new arrivals light their candles from those of the people already there. Where did they get all the candles? They must have paid dearly for them.

In the center of the clearing a gigantic stearin-candle has been placed on a thick stump which is meant to represent the altar. Even in the flickering lights of the candles one can see that these worshippers have donned whatever decent clothes they still have left. Under the drab fur coats there are flashes of brightly colored blouses and peasant smocks.

The congregation stands in respectful silence waiting for the service to begin. Father Nikolai has disappeared among the trees somewhere to get ready. Finally a dignified old man in a long white beard wearing a dazzling white shirt under his open padded jacket takes his place at the altar. With his beard and beetling white eyebrows he looks like Tolstoy. Filling the office of deacon, he opens a huge volume and begins to read resonantly from the Book of Acts. As he reads, an extemporaneous choir lines up behind him.

The reading continues for some time. I see that the deacon's hands are beginning to tremble from holding up the heavy Bible. All around me the worshippers are crossing themselves and whispering fervent but unintelligible prayers. Tolstoy ends his reading just as Father Nikolai, garbed in black, makes his appearance. Holding his cross aloft with his left hand and swinging his censer with his right, the priest proceeds to walk around the congregation in a slow and stately manner. As fragrant fumes of incense waft through the multitude, he chants in his high, melodious voice:

"Your Resurrection, Christ Redeemer, is sung by the angels in heaven. Help us also here on earth to praise You with pure hearts."

Now he stops and faces in a westerly direction. I recall this is meant to represent the vigil before the locked door of the tomb.

Then the priest proclaims loudly: "Christ has risen from the dead, through death has conquered death and brought life even to those in the grave."

At this point the choir breaks forth, while the priest triumphantly repeats his proclamation. He raises his cross once more and with his censer makes the sign of the cross over the door of the tomb. He steps to the candle-altar as the hymn swells to majestic volume: "Christ is risen from the dead."

The peasant worshippers fall to the ground and cross themselves again and again in an ecstasy of adoration.

I am deeply stirred by what is happening in the Russian soul here before my eyes. The ritual is alien to me, but there is no denying its power. Certainly these suffering peasants are lifted up and carried away by it. Not one of them is holding back; no one stands by indifferently.

The choir is now singing "Christ is Risen from the Dead," St. John Damascene's mighty canon. While the basses sound the depths of the ocean, the sopranos soar through the skies with the joyful news: " . . . is risen—is risen—is risen."

Now the imposing deacon, face transfigured, lifts the great candle from the stump and walks around the congregation, followed by the priest with his cross and censer.

"*Khristos voskress!* Christ is risen!" Father Nikolai repeats again in a strong voice to the assembled and looks over in my direction.

The choir swells to a glorious climax, "Let us embrace and kiss each other, brethern! And by the power of the Resurrection—" here the voices thunder in exaltation, "forgive those who hate us."

In an instant the mass of worshippers breaks up. "*Khristos voskress!*" sounds from hundreds of throats. Everywhere people are embracing, laughing, shouting. "*Voistinno voskress!* Has risen indeed!" The beads of candlelight dance in the darkness. Wretched, half-starved prisoners are rejoicing, wary strangers become loving brothers and sisters. Russians are celebrating Easter here in the frozen, primeval northern forest.

I can't stand on the sidelines a moment longer; I spring from the shadows and mix joyously, zestfully with the other celebrants. Everywhere happy, weeping faces seek the conforting reassurance of physical contact, the sweet balm of kisses. I see a young mother ecstatically embracing her pathetically thin, half-starved son, then turn and impulsively shower kisses on an old woman who may be her mother, or aunt, or just a fellow human sufferer.

Gradually, the hugging and kissing subside. Once more Father Nikolai takes his place at the altar and patiently waits for his worshippers to coalesce into a congregation again. His sermon is short and to the point.

"Dear adherents of the true faith, brothers and sisters! We have assembled here for an Easter celebration in rather different circumstances than we are used to. Where is the church? Where are the bells? Where our accustomed divine service?

"In His incomprehensible wisdom, God has led us into an Easterless time, so that He can make the Resurrection of His Son live for us in quite a different way than heretofore. You saw how, instead of walking around the church, I prescribed a circle around you all. *You* are the church here! Instead of bells pealing, *yours* are the living voices which bear witness to the miracle of miracles.

"Be of courage even when you are forced to sacrifice your lives in the savage wilderness of the north. We have borne witness to His Resurrection even here. You may be forced to perish, but not one of you will be lost—for Christ is risen! Go back to your harsh routine, ready to die but still happy, rich in your poverty as lost lambs found by the Lord. *Khristos voskress!*"

"*Voistinno voskress!* the congregation answers as one.

It is still dark when I begin the long walk home alone. Father Nikolai has decided to stay with his celebrants a little longer. I feel exhausted, but cleansed and buoyant in my soul. A Mennonite celebrating an Orthodox Easter mass at night in the middle of the northern forest! And why not? This is my reality now; Mariental is a fading dream.

When spring finally comes to the North it comes dramatically, with a rush, as though making up for lost time. Two hundred days of winter have held this world in thrall. Then, in the delicate pause between April and May, frost-stunned nature begins to stir and stretch. One day a mild southwind comes fluttering in, softening the ice and dissolving the snow. Wild geese, swans, and wild ducks return again. From the Far North the polar fox glides down, driven by the scrabble in his belly. Herds of reindeer, pursued by great black clouds of mosquitoes, follow their amphibious routes north by land and river guided by the wild and resourceful Samoyeds,[6] who are hunters, fishermen, and self-appointed herdsmen to the reindeer. They keep their northern preserves under control by constructing strategically placed pitfalls and building and maintaining wild game fences.

During the night of April thirtieth a warm breeze rustles around the barrack. The roof groans and water comes trickling through the cracks. The trees are soughing a playful parody of human voices. I listen sleepless in my bunk. A feeling of excitement, a singing in the blood such as I have not felt in a long time, suffuses my being.

The others in our barrack seem to be affected also. I hear coughing and whispering. The bunks are creaking more than usual. The children mutter and squirm in an uneasy half-sleep.

Something is happening. I feel oddly different, almost transformed. I toss and turn, but sleep is gone. These squalid surroundings, to which I have sullenly grown accustomed, are suddenly unbearable again. My restlessness urgently demands movement, action, release. Impulsively, I jump up and fumble on my clothes in the dark. Suddenly a tremendous burst of thunder rolls through the forest. Then another—Cra—aa—aa—ck. The echoes continue to spread through the trees as I open the door and feel the warm, moist night air on my face. I know Wolff and Tielmann will follow me outside. They saw me dressing and in moments were reaching for their own clothes.

As if by pre-arranged plan, the three of us fall into step and start walking westward towards the river. We are driven by a common impulse, to get away—anywhere from the fetid, stifling prison we are forced to call home.

Another mighty clap of thunder undulates through the landscape followed by a loud, prolonged splintering sound like as if all the glass in the world were smashing at once.

"Hey, that's not thunder, "Wolff cries. "That's the river ice breaking up. Come on, let's take a look. It's supposed to be quite a sight."

[6]These are a Ural-Altaic people who live in northwestern Siberia and along the northeastern coast of the Soviet Union.

We hurry along through the melting snow, which has fused into a dirty mush that gives soddenly with every step. Where the tree line ends we find puddles and pools dotting the uneven moor. Fortunately most of the pools are shallow; nevertheless, our feet are soon sopping wet.

"So, it's spring at last," Tielmann observes as he narrowly misses another black puddle. "Now we can sell our fur coats."

"We'd be better off just to rest them a bit. We'll be needing them again before you can sing 'The Last Rose of Summer,' " Wolff cracks.

A large crowd has gathered on the banks of the Mezen. People we recognize from the kitchen queues call out greetings. The crowd is in a jovial mood, as though celebrating a public holiday.

We have arrived just in time to witness an awesome drama of nature. The eerie stage-lights of the polar night are perfect for the spectacle. Like a primordial Titan awakening from sleep, the Mezen is heaving up its thick covering of ice. The gigantic blocks rear up like sea monsters, black and threatening, crash together, grind and splinter each other, split and crumble along their deep gashes, and settle with heavy splashes into the roaring channel. Then gradually the jagged floes lock horns and begin to form an immense ice dam which pushes out far beyond the banks on either side. Great hulks of ice come ploughing savagely into the soft banks like mortally wounded bulls.

For the first time the audience is directly involved in the drama. With the dark waters beginning to rise behind the dam, the crowd breaks up in alarm and disperses up the bank. At what they consider a safe distance they stop to await the next scene. After awhile the waters, hissing and rampant, come surging over the snowy banks. In no time the raging flood has climbed the dam itself and hurtles over, a torrential waterfall, to the fissured ice-floor below. Another cra-aa-ck rips through the dam, the sound howling away through the night. As if they had been dynamited, masses of ice are hurled into the air. Again the primeval forest sends back a mighty echo. The dam is breached; it sags and then collapses with an unearthly roar. Quickly, the renegade waters swirl back into their accustomed riverbed.

We continue to watch for a long time, as reluctant to leave as a theatre audience after a good play. We feel emotionally purged by this exuberant, reckless display of primitive power, by this extravagant promise of the coming of spring and of renewed life even in the midst of this wintry desolation. We may be prisoners here, but even Fur Cap and the State cannot control the cyclical movement of the seasons, nor prevent the sheer exultation, the surge of new hope in the breasts of their hapless victims. And we are all—victims and oppressors alike—equally helpless in the face of an everchanging world whose natural rhythms are controlled by a higher power than any that man can muster.

In early May I receive a letter from abroad. My mother's nephew in Wuertemburg has answered my letter. His tone is honest and affectionate and he has some heart-warming things to say:

. . . Your unexpected letter gave us much pleasure, but it has also shocked us profoundly. We are ready to do anything we can to assist you and to bring the plight of all of you to public attention. Believe me, we will do everything in our power to rescue our own flesh and blood.

As for an official investigation, we can't count on that. Our politics are also determined by economic conditions. It is an open secret that the lumber which you are paying for with your health and lives in northern Russia and Siberia is being sold here in great volume at scandalously low prices. In fact, it can be bought at a lower price than our own lumber from the Alps. What is even worse is that the general public seems strangely indifferent to that fact, and to the picture in general.

I shall make inquiries at the post office today and send you whatever I am permitted. You can rest easy; we won't forget you . . . .

We all send you our best wishes, including Jacob, who resides in Stuttgart and Ernst, who has a farm in Hesse.

With love,

F. and E. Hahn.

For the rest of the day I am in a state of euphoria. I pour over every word of the letter again and again. How long has it been since I have received a letter that breathes such humanity, such love—and from a person I have never met!

In the evening I proudly read my letter to the others in Number Seven. They are moved to tears by its cheering contents.

Well—!" I turned triumphantly to Wolff. "This should thaw even your pessimism. You can see that spring has truly arrived."

"Yes," Wolff counters, "but the night frosts aren't over. Let's wait. What you should really take to heart is the friendly information that we are supplying skilled labor, so to speak, for Western Europe. In any case," he concludes wickedly, "it's comforting to know that we are providing housing materials for the more civilized people."

Hans Neufeld, of course, has to add his own acrid comment. "Even if they supported us completely from over there, it wouldn't atone for this filthy business of cheap lumber. They're exploiting us like slaves, the fat swine!" He utters a string of Russian obscenities and storms out of the barrack in one of his black rages.

Penner has obtained permission from "Comma", as Tielmann calls him, for us to put in a vegetable garden.

"Of course, first we'll have to find out what will grow here—if anything—"

"—Ah, yes," Wolff is at it again, "everything will depend on whether we employ proper agricultural methods. With proper planting, careful cultivation—voilà! we can export another product. That's what we're here for, after all, to serve the State, to work for the common good of all."

"Volodya," I plead, "just for once, give us a chance to plan something without making it sound absurd."

Wolff pretends to be contrite. "May one be permitted to ask for how long a period this model farm is to operate? In the end you may create a rustic paradise here you won't want to leave. And then they'll have to exile you all the way to the North Pole to punish you for your *kulak*-like activities."

Even dour old Penner is forced to smile.

By next day we have settled on a plan. We decide to cultivate the soil in the cleared part of the forest. As the gardening is to be done largely by the women who remain at home, they will be unable to remove the larger stumps and will simply have to sow around and between them. We men must continue to work in the forest in order to get full rations.

The following morning Penner, who is making himself responsible for the garden project, collects a small sum of money from the rest of us and goes off to Andreievka to purchase spades and seeds. The women, with a little help from some of us, spend the day trying to remove as many of the smaller stumps as they can. Next day the women set to work even more enthusiastically, first spading the spongy forest loam and then putting in a crop of carrots, radishes, and sunflowers. The two Preuss girls are spared from their tree-pruning to help the other women with the gardening. Theresa Preuss, who has been reluctantly coming to work with us for the last while, doesn't bother to disguise her eagerness to be excused from the job. She seems to jump at every excuse for getting out of the forest work.

The women sing softly as they work. It's a pleasant and reassuring sound to hear in the cutting area. Perhaps things really will get better this summer.

Ohm Peters returns from the hospital. He is weak but at least free of malaria. He remains in his bunk reading and meditating, but he is cheerful and uncomplaining. On Saturday evening, after we get home, he shuffles over to the stove (which we still heat because of the cold nights) and invites us all to a reading from his dilapidated Bible.

For a few precious moments a brighter, nobler world stands before us, one that is comforting but also saddening when we contrast it with the reality of our oppressive prison life. The utter meaninglessness of our daily routine has a deadening effect on our spiritual lives. The flashes of hope we derive from our primitive worship services are growing weaker and less frequent. More and more we are succumbing to the sin of apathy. I confess this freely to Ohm Jasch.

He refuses to be discouraged. "We'll all be awakened at last," he says with gentle conviction.

One day in early May Penner collapses on the job. Malaria. We carry him back to the barracks. We report to Comma's office and make urgent pleas to borrow the horse and wagon, but all in vain. The horse is being used somewhere and is not available. In desperation I make the rounds of the inmates and try to collect something more to add to my last three rubles. I finally manage to get together nineteen rubles and a few kopeks. I take the money to the Cossack. He grins and assures me that the horse and wagon will be at my disposal within the hour. As I leave he puts his finger to his mouth. He does not want Comma to know.

There is nothing for it. I am obliged to sacrifice a full day of work in order to take the sick man to Andreievka. The trip proves to be refreshing. Once again I can feast my eyes on cultivated fields. They are small and have been wrested from the forest floor. The Zyrian peasants do their wood-cutting in the fall and leave the cut logs, except for the larger trunks, lying in the clearings through the winter. In May, when the spring sun has dried them, they burn the logs and then plough under the ashes. In this soil they sow their barley and rye.

Our garden comes up very spotty, but at least we can now look at some tender young shoots on our way to and from work. How pathetic all this is, though, compared with the vast stretches of vigorously sprouting fields we had back home. And yet, those pictures of the past are slowly beginning to fade. Is it just the passing of time, or are our memories becoming enfeebled along with our bodies?

No matter how much we need our camp bathhouse after our week's dirty work in the forest, it is becoming a hazardous place for us. In Number Eight half the inmates, including the Bergens, are suffering from scabies. Even worse, we are getting our first cases of scurvy. In our Number Seven Tielmann is again the first to get it. He becomes very weak and develops ugly lumps on his body; his gums bleed constantly and his back is a huge tracery of broken blood vessels. A few days later Father Nikolai is forced to stay in bed.

Koehn and I decide to "rent" the horse and wagon again. But we don't know where to raise the funds. We appeal to Wolff. In an emergency he can be serious and helpful.

It doesn't take him long to come up with a solution. "Listen, fellows, we have to purchase our own horse."

We stare at him.

"No, look—it'll be cheaper in the long run than to keep paying rent money. And when the time comes we can slaughter it for food, for the winter." He slaps my knee as if that settles the matter.

"The money?" I query.

"The barter system, old chap. That's the fashionable thing around here." He goes to his bunk. "Here's my fur coat; who'll throw in his?" He thumps his good greatcoat down at our feet.

"I'll put in my fur jacket."

"*Khorosho.* Koehn—why don't you do the collecting? With your expert knowledge of horseflesh you'll act as our purchasing agent, in any case. So, let's go. Long live the socialized economy of the voluntary resettlers in Camp 513!"

As he rummages around in his chest for other items, Wolff whistles the Communist funeral march.

I can see it's a good plan. The Zyrian peasants have been stubbornly resisting compulsory collectivization. We are witnessing the same scene here we played out in our colonies in 'twenty-nine.[7] The peasants are selling off their livestock dirt cheap for money or clothing, so that when the collective

[7]This year marked the end of the relatively liberal New Economic Policy (1921-29) and the beginning of Stalin's brutal new tactics to enforce collectivization all over the Soviet Union.

farms do become a reality the people will bring nothing to them but still have the means to buy food for awhile.

Yes, it's a good time for us to buy a horse, but we'll also have to find a place to keep it. Koehn suggests that we let some peasant nearby keep it and use it for the feeding whenever we don't require its services.

By next day everything has been arranged. Koehn has purchased a horse and a battered old wagon for a pile of fur coats, jackets, pants, and a very small amount of cash. We entrust the outfit to a reliable Zyrian trapper who lives four kilometers away. Koehn assumes the part-time duties of driver. The rest of us will make up his reduced bread ration.

Our transportation facility begins to pay off immediately. One after the other of our group is stricken by malaria. The patients are taken directly to Andreievka by Koehn. Each time he and the patients have to listen to the same painful (and futile) advice by the doctor or his assistant—namely, that we should follow a better diet. But when Koehn tries to explain our situation to them they turn away and pretend not to hear or understand.

Our ranks continue to grow thinner, and Koehn's ambulance is kept busy. On June tenth Penner is released from hospital, but returns to the forest only as a part-time worker. Then Neufeld gets sick and is taken to hospital. Koehn is no sooner back when he is forced to return to Andreievka with Theresa Preuss, who is definitely not feigning illness this time. A few days later Mrs. Preuss is taken in with a case of scurvy, but is sent home again after a day or two. Next, Koehn has to take his own wife to the hospital; she is suffering from an ugly skin rash combined with a high fever. The remaining women look after the three Koehn children when they are not in nursery school. Finally, a desperate Bergen from next door persuades Koehn to take his wife and child to the hospital.

The rest of us sink into an even deeper state of apathy. By day we work slowly, listlessly, like sleepwalkers. We no longer try to outwit the guards by snatching conversation breaks at every opportunity. In the evenings we fall directly into our bunks, without bothering with the little shared personal tasks which constitute much of our social life. Even Martha and Wolff no longer spend much time together. Martha devotes her free time to her mother now that Theresa is in the hospital. The two are longing for a rest day so they can visit the sick girl.

Yes, our resilient spring mood of a month ago is gone. The buoyancy we felt then was based on the false assumption that we could share in nature's annual spring renewal. But the outlook of sickness and disease among us is a forcible reminder of just how vulnerable we are in this place. To add to our woes, our runty forest garden is struck by a series of late frosts in mid-June which kill a large part of the fragile young plants. And it would be futile to put in a second crop. Summer ends in August here.

"By the time a new crop is up the fall frosts will be here," Koehn judges, correctly as it turns out.

On the twentieth of June we get our first rest day in a month. Fatigued though we are, Koehn, Wolff, and I simply can't stay in our bunks. Since the weather is fairly warm and sunny, we decide to go for a walk in the direction of the Zyrian villages. We long to get away, as far away as possible, from the infernal trees and barracks, from all the people whose misery and suffering are stamped so blatantly on their emaciated faces!

Away from our dulling environment I look at my two companions more objectively. The dramatic part in Wolff's beard has almost disappeared in a luxurious mass of curls. He looks positively professorial, but he has grown quieter, has lost some of his verbal effervescence. Koehn's blond beard is still wispy and pointed, but now laced with grey. He too has lost some of the spontaneous warmth and vitality which have always drawn me to him. But he is still the strongest, the most durable among us, I suspect. I wonder if the other two are aware of how sluggish our movements are? We are shuffling along like feeble old men.

Koehn stops to whittle himself a birch sapling to use as a walking stick. He pretends that it is merely a sentimental gesture. "It's to help me recapture the feeling of being back in the village again on a lazy Sunday afternoon looking over the young crops," he says a little sheepishly.

Wolff nods but says nothing.

Near the edge of the forest we come upon the broad clearings where the Zyrian settlements stand. The villages look miserably poor. A few of the thatched roofs boast roughly carved horsehead weathervanes, perhaps the modest indicators of less depressed times. Near the villages there are fields of new rye. The seed has sprouted unevenly. The crops stand fairly thick and tall in the center but are very sparse around the edges.

Beside the road lies the trunk of a huge mountain ash. It is long enough and thick enough to enable the three of us to lie down on it in a row. With the sun smiling down we close our eyes . . ..

Memories of Sunday afternoons in Mariental come flooding back. Along the outlying village paths, in the cool shade of the yellow acacias, the local Mordvinians[8] used to play and dance their strange, hypnotic songs. Their long white smocks would swirl under bright girdles as the dancers leaped and curled and stamped imperiously in ever-changing patterns of movement and color. Their tunes and rhythms are embedded in my soul forever. By contrast, the Mennonite farmyards were hushed and empty in the solemnity of a rural Sunday—so different from the gaiety around them. I remember animals and machines all decently removed from sight . . . parents sedately napping in the *eckstube*, digesting the heavy, cold Sunday dinner . . . small children morosely inactive, fighting the stillness . . . yards neatly raked, all doors respectfully closed . . . around the shed the impudent cackle of a stray chicken or two . . . the high summer sun pouring down over the nodding fields . . . indolent strains of the balalaika caressing the silence . . .

"—Wake up!" Koehn shatters my daydream. Startled, I throw open my eyes.

Koehn is disturbed and nervously hurls his stick out into the field.

"Did you have a nice dream—about the old days?" Wolff demands facetiously.

[8]These are a race of people living in the upper Volga region who speak a Finno-Ugric language and are Orthodox Christians.

Koehn's face is tense. "I just can't shake it. When I'm dozing like that, it all comes back again . . .. I can't take it—let's not talk about it."

Towards the end of June I receive notice that a shipment from abroad has arrived for me at the post office. I am requested to pick it up within the week. The package will be released only to the addressee personally.

Before I am back from the post office Comma is inquiring for me. I report to him as soon as I get back.

"Tell me, citizen," he opens ominously, "why was this foreign package sent to you?"

"I—I have relatives there."

"Hmm. Have they ever sent you packages containing foodstuffs before?"

"Comrade—Citizen Commandant," I amend respectfully, "I don't know whether the package contains foodstuffs; I haven't had a chance to open it yet."

Comma realizes his error and looks a trifle embarrassed. "All right," he continues briskly, "how do your—relatives, as you claim, know what to send you? Obviously, you must have complained to them." His sly grin is to indicate that he has turned the tables.

"I didn't complain—just . . . sort of . . . described the situation."

"And how many others have 'just sort of described the situation' "—he is enjoying his own sarcasm—"considering that over forty such packages arrived in my district today?"

My heart leaps, but I try not to give away anything. "I know nothing about that; I can't answer for the others."

His tone goes hard. "And just what kind of foreign organization supports your *begging* ring?"

"I know nothing, Citizen Commandant."

His eyes narrow to steel slits. "Tell me something. Can the people over there afford to support you here?"

"Well, apparently—or they wouldn't be sending the packages," I venture cautiously.

"Then why don't they help their own seven million unemployed people with such *packages*?" His rising tone is triumphant.

I'm at a loss. "Well . . . I wouldn't know about that. But I assume they are doing that too," I end lamely.

He's enjoying himself now. "Ha-ha—'you assume they are doing that too,' " he mimics. "Don't be a damn fool, *germanets*. We know how to deal with your kind."

The interview is getting too warm for comfort. There is only one way out. "Citizen Commandant, with your permission, I would like—so to speak—to give you a sort of sample, or *proof*," I correct myself, "of Western friendship—this evening, when I've had a chance to—"

"All right, all right—good, good—" he gets my point. He gestures with his hand. The interrogation is over.

The address on the package is that of my uncle in Heilbronn. The German postmark shows the date of dispatch as March seventh. The battery of Russian stamps that surrounds it gives visible proof of how the package has wandered from place to place—at least partly due to the badly copied Russian address. Still, three months from Wuertemburg to Vologda is a long time.

I open the package. A note that had been clearly pasted to the inside cover has been removed. I remember something. I dig into the bottom of the carton and find a duplicate of the list of contents. Covering the list—a clutch of small stones!

I consult the list. "Two sets of underwear"—yes, on top. "One winter shirt"—yes. "Two pairs woollen socks"—yes—no! I find only one pair. And that's all I find. I run over the rest of the list: "One and a half kilograms of wheat flour, a half kilogram of sugar, three pieces of soap"—all missing. I cursed silently. How I could have used all the missing articles on the list! Well, at least I have some underwear, a shirt, and socks for the coming winter.

I report back to Comma. "Citizen Commandant, I'm afraid the package contains only a few personal articles of clothing—mainly underwear and socks. I—I won't be able to keep my promise after all."

"Only articles of clothing?" he echoes in mock astonishment, and turns away in dismissal.

During the course of the summer Wolff receives several letters from his family, which has found a home of sorts in Siberia. The letters are written by his sister, who has married a German engineer there. One day he reads me part of his latest letter.

. . . You will be amazed to hear that on May 27th twins were born to us. In spite of everything, joy, great joy. After all, even this is according to Scripture: "the more pharoah oppressed the people, the more they increased"—or words to that effect.[9] But then our constant fears for tomorrow torment us again. We have to stretch our bread so carefully. In spite of Victor's better job, we barely survive.

Uncle Waldemar died peacefully the day before yesterday. We say "peacefully" now as a matter of course, for death is considered by most of us here as a blessing. And in Uncle's case this was true in a special sense. On his deathbed he received an order to report to the G.P.U. Had he survived he would have shared your fate—even at his age.

The famine—just before the harvest, even among the farming population—is reaching frightening proportions. In Slavograd our people have in many cases devoured the last dog, and even mice and rats.

Sometimes I wonder which place is worse—yours up north or ours here—Wolff breaks off, his eyes glistening.

[9]But the more they afflicted them, the more they multiplied and grew." (Exodus 1:12)

Our patients, in various states of convalescence, are back with us again. Mrs. Koehn and Hans Neufeld are still not strong enough to do anything. Tielmann is ailing badly with the terrible rabies on his hands, but he grimly puts in his regular shift in the forest. Theresa Preuss is back with her mother, who is looking more gaunt and infirm than ever. The bloom is gone from the girl's face and she has lost weight, but seems well again otherwise. She seems to be in no hurry to go back to work, though, and waits on her mother as though nothing else mattered. She also starts taking long walks to the Command Post—to get back her strength she says.

The young Mrs. Bergen and her infant son do not return from the hospital. Bergen takes their loss very hard. In his distracted state he insists on taking Ohm Peters to Andreievka with him to preside over the burial. Later, when we ask Bergen where his wife and child are buried he is evasive and will tell us only that they are buried "in a safe place in the forest." Ohm Peters makes Bergen his special concern, but it takes the poor man a long time to get over his grief.

Almost every day on our way to work we stop for a few moments to see how our garden is doing.

"Look how nicely the radishes are coming along, Vladimir Ivanovitch," Martha Preuss says one morning, pointing to the erect rows of greenery.

"Very nice," Wolff praises, "but you know, actually I don't care much for radishes."

Don't care for—?"

"—No, I'm suspicious of them—so red on the outside, so white on the inside." That sounds more like the old Wolff, I think with a smile.

Martha also looks pleased, "Ah, you still have some of your irony left, I see."

"When you've spent the better part of a year in this place, Marfa Petrovna, you're lucky if you have much of anything left."

During the summer months we have been allowed to work under less stringent supervision. As a result we have organized the work among ourselves in such a way that each of us works at only one phase of the operation in felling, de-branching, peeling, sawing, or piling. This division of labor makes the work considerably easier for all of us.

On the other hand, the daily work norms for absentees now have to be made up by the rest of us. When we are all there we have an easy time of it, with lots of time for conversation and smoke-breaks. But on days when several people are missing (our convalescents are counted as absentees) we are forced to work almost without interruption. Thus, much of the time we still work in a mood of near-desperation. And our mood is not helped by our dread of the coming winter. Our fear of a second winter here is almost harder to bear than the scabies and the scurvy.

Only Father Nikolai and Ohm Peters never seem to lose their iron calm. Both have an inner serenity which makes the rest of us seek their company.

In the evenings I find conversing with Ohm Jasch more restful than lying in my bunk. During the daytime I like to be near the priest, who irradiates the work site with his homespun Russian wisdom. He is very much in the tradition of Dostoevsky's Father Sosima in *The Brothers Karamazov*. Almost certainly the last of his line, I realize sadly.

The weeks just before harvest are especially bad. For months now the bread ration for the workers has been reduced by forty grams to four hundred and sixty grams per day. The twenty grams of oil are distributed only every fourth day and the promised ten grams of sugar are missing completely.

My daily cubic centimeter of bread. I hold it in my hand and stare at it. Bread—the staff of life. This is the meagre thing that millions of people in this vast, fruitful land are obliged to toil for daily in unspeakable conditions, browbeaten and oppressed by callous brutes who care only about stuffing their own guts. Unimaginable misery, degradation, shame—all for a measly hunk of adulterated black bread. Bread, bitter bread—for your sake men lie, betray, steal, slander, and even murder. Russia and bread. The sacred bread of Little Mother Russia. What an essay that would make: the historical, and mystical, significance of *khleb* in Russia. No, the subject would require volumes. Bread *is* the history of our country.

To their great surprise, the Koehns receive a small, wooden chest from our home village. Koehn rips it open eagerly. It is packed with flour.

"This must be the modern form of Elijah's ravens," he jokes happily.

"Yes," Wolff adds, "the modern form is getting just enough bread to stay alive—but no meat. Old Elijah got both. We'd be glad to devour even the ravens if we could."

We are not given our next rest day until well into July. Again the three of us go for a walk in the fields. The rye is beginning to ripen. We lie down on the edge of a field and gaze at close-range into the forest of ears waving in the breeze, bumping each other playfully, whispering their tiny secrets. I pull an ear from its stalk, but the kernels look anemic and soft, scarcely developed. They aren't worth chewing on. Disappointed, we search the wild grass and find some sorrel plants. Wolff also finds some dandelions.

The breeze wafts the fragrance of ripening grain over us. "That's the smell of Russia—mother, whore, murderess!" Wolff shouts as if drunk.

Koehn gets up. "Come on, let's walk around the field."

"So you can play landowner one more time?" Wolff says, not without a touch of malice.

But Koehn ignores him. He runs his practised eye over the undulating waves of rye. That's how I used to see him at home. We walk slowly, as if lost in thought. Or are we just weary?

Nearby there is a stand of long-eared barley; it is stunted and thin-looking. In single file we walk along its edge, Wolff in the lead. As he walks, he trails his hand over the nodding ears, then scoops up their warm scent and breathes it in deeply.

"Stop!" Wolff bends down. Over his shoulder I see a child sprawled in the grass: a pale little girl with hollow cheeks and half-open mouth, clutching a bunch of barley ears.

Wolff lifts the child carefully, then puts her down again. The tattered little smock is thread-bare; the tiny feet are barely covered by unbelievably ragged button-shoes.

"She's dead, probably starved," Koehn remarks superfluously.

Wolff is visibly upset. "Let's get out of this place," he grates, and turns away quickly.

In mid-summer, our convalescents go out in the fields daily to pick grasses and leaves, especially sorrel. In the forest there are mushrooms, which they gather by the pailful. They also pick willow leaves, which after a few cooking experiments turn out to be quite tasty. Since our carefully hoarded supplies of flour are dwindling, we decide not to bake supplementary bread out of pure flour anymore. Instead, we mix the flour with mushrooms and leaves. To one pail of greens or mushrooms we add two cups of flour. We eat this mixture in considerable quantities with our noontime soup, but all it does is fill the stomach; we remain gassily hungry.

The names and addresses of people in Germany are being circulated through Camp 513. The inmates are now writing regular weekly begging letters. Wolff refers to them as "country cousin" letters. The closer we get to winter the more apprehensive, if not desperate, we become. Everyone who still has the price of a postcard is busy writing. We are beyond caring what the recipients will think of us. We know that our survival this winter will depend on food packages from abroad.

Willie Koehn finds one of Penner's postcards on the road to Yenisseievka. It is dirty and torn and minus its postage stamp.

"Letter unacceptable," is Neufeld's guess.

We often wonder how many of our cards are being rejected by the authorities or going astray in transit. It is a fragile lifeline which may be cut at any time. All we can do is hope and pray.

It doesn't help our morale to note that service at the post office is becoming increasingly erratic. It happens frequently that somebody will receive notification of a parcel having arrived for him, only to find that there has been an error and that the shipment is meant for an identically named post office in Siberia and, by an even greater coincidence, for someone of the same name. We don't know whether to attribute this sort of thing to corruption within the post office or to the endless duplication of Russian place names and Mennonite family names. Probably a combination of both, which doesn't make it any less frustrating.

One day Tielmann receives notice of a package. The welcome news lifts him out of his doldrums; he decides to fetch it immediately. We try to talk him out of it because it will be nighttime long before he gets there. He refuses to listen and sets off.

The post office is closed. He finally locates the postmaster who agrees to hand over the parcel but only if Tielmann pays the "duty."

"Do you have money for the duty?"

"Money for the duty?" Tielmann is dumbfounded.

"Those are my instructions: individual foodstuffs and items of clothing are subject to fixed rates of duty."

Tielmann is still at sea. Finally he blurts: "I haven't got a single kopek!"

"That's too bad. Then you'll have to pay value in kind."

"How much?"

"According to what the parcel contains."

"—What the parcel contains?" Tielmann echoes weakly.

They open the package. In addition to a heavy wool jacket, it contains two and a half kilograms of flour, a kilogram of rice, and three-quarters of a kilogram of bacon. The postmaster calculates this way and that. Finally he declares he will accept the two and a half kilograms of flour.

"Evgeni Igorovitch," Tielmann tries to compromise, "Why don't you take one kilogram of flour, half of the rice, and half of the bacon? Try to put yourself in my place . . .."

"Good enough!" The postmaster waves magnanimously.

Tielmann divides the contents.

"You're lucky," the postmaster observes placidly. "Not all shipments arrive so intact."

Tielmann says he understands.

He donates the flour to our common larder. Mrs. Koehn has taken over the baking. The children stand around the oven and bombard her with questions.

"Will we get some bread too?"

"Of course."

"Why do you bake with leaves, Mama?"

"We don't have enough flour."

"Will the bread taste better that way?"

No answer.

"Why can't we have proper bread—like at home?"

Again no answer.

The five hungry children continue to ask their innocently cruel questions. Their hollow eyes are fixed on the rolled-out dough and they follow every movement. The gaunt little cheeks take on a little color from the heat of the stove and the thought of fresh bread.

"The bread in the nursery school tastes better," the little Albrecht lad pipes up.

Mrs. Koehn pricks up her ears. "Why is it better?"

"Well, it just tastes better. And when I know the Revolutionary songs well, I always get more bread. It tastes a lot better!"

"Do you always know the songs well enough?"

"When I'm hungry I learn them faster."

"Oh."

The boy, through some childish intuition, suddenly realizes that he has said too much and drifts away.

The harvest brings no visible relief to our lives. Once again, we are driven to collect whatever clothing we can spare to barter for food. Actually, with winter just around the corner, we are surrendering clothes that we can't really spare.

For two days I prowl around the neighborhood bartering clothes, blankets, and footwear for whatever foodstuffs I can find. My leather boots complete with rubber overshoes are worth twenty kilograms of flour. Mrs. Penner's large woollen shawl brings thirty kilograms. For an apron I receive ten kilograms of rye meal.

So we struggle through one more food crisis.

What is equally distressing is that the work conditions have been tightened up. The administration has reorganized our logging operations. Comma has divided us into work units which he calls crews. This means that the work is now rigidly standardized; each worker has to cut or peel three cubic meters per day. At the transportation end of the operation each man with his team is responsible for nine cubic meters per day.

Thus, our more flexible, self-organized system of divided labor has been eliminated. Any production above the prescribed norm has no effect on the size of the rations. But anyone who does not meet the new work norm is to have a corresponding reduction in his ration.

"So, we tighten our belts another notch, if that's still possible for anyone," Koehn says bitterly. "At this rate none of us will last much longer."

"We may as well barter our belts now," Wolff adds grimly.

"While we still have them," growls Neufeld.

Penner has heard at the camp kitchen that as part of the work detail reorganization Comma is obliged to clothe every forest worker completely.

"With what," Neufeld demands bluntly, "curses and sarcasm?"

That evening Wolff goes to make some inquiries. He brings back the news that tomorrow work pants are to be distributed to all male workers, although only on loan. The clothes are to remain state property and must be returned when the "season" is over.

"That means when we no longer require them," is Wolff's sardonic interpretation.

In early September we get our first heavy frosts. The temperature at night plummets to minus twenty-nine. But in spite of everything, there is still a little laughter (grim) and bantering (hard-edged) in our crew when we set out for work in the morning. I have the uneasy feeling that we have passed the stage of routine gallows humor and are now becoming morbid and dangerously unbalanced. Only Wolff seems to retain some sense of proportion in his joking.

Tielmann is wearing his new woolen jacket. His fur coat, like that of most of us, has long since been bartered for food.

"Fur coats and the like are a denial of socialist ideology, in any case," Wolff begins in his best style. "I can't understand why the state still allows such capitalistic items of clothing to be worn. Just look at Tielmann. State-owned pants below the equator, a proper *kulak* jacket above, and the two mismatched parts held together by a neutral rope-belt. But, of course, gentlemen, we are living in an age of symbolism. Consider. Tielmann represents the struggling powers of the world: he walks around in Communism—just look how he strides along. That's the giant's stride of total collectivization. The jacket! Well now, that's capitalistic Europe—bound to us by a slack stretchy rope of international commerce."

Koehn surprises us by reporting that our trapper is unwilling to feed our horse through the winter. He wants to be rid of it as soon as possible. We discuss the problem carefully and decide to slaughter the animal.

"It's really the only thing we can do," Koehn argues.

Penner's suggestion that we sell it is rejected by the rest of us on the grounds that prices are too low. Butchering for meat is the only answer.

On the way home we are already thinking about the meat, a commodity we have not seen for a long time. No doubt each of us is privately calculating what his share of the meat will be and how best to utilize it and make it last.

Next day we butcher. Once again we are kept going by a flicker of hope in our northern night.

Part Three
Escape The Wild Wind

Above my bunk hangs a tiny advertising calendar which one of the children brought to me from nursery school. The pad is no more than three by five centimeters and the paper of poor quality. The slightly larger upper panel depicts a model collective farm in garish colors.

"Why shouldn't our glorious new age be as publicized as the old one was?" Tielmann remarks when he sees the calendar. "All those Revolutionary holidays marked in bright red! And we used to think the Old Style calendar had a lot of state and church holidays and feast days."

Every morning I tear off the date page and put it in my pocket. Just in case somebody asks me for the date. My little calendar and I come in for all kinds of facetious comments.

"Listen, Professor," Wolff starts off from his bunk one evening, "do you know why your calendar is showing red tomorrow?"

I try to ignore him, but he repeats the question.

I turn and look at him warily.

Gleefully he answers his own question. "Because tomorrow is the memorable day on which fate decided to propel you into this wicked world. It's your birthday, man, if I recall correctly!"

Volodya—shut up!"

"*Khorosho, khorosho,* but look here, it's a kind of political predestination to have your birthday fall on a red-letter day. Yeah, that's a good one!" he chuckles. "Look at it this way: if you weren't here, you could always celebrate your birthday on a holiday. We'd be free to celebrate it together. Remember how we used to sail along the Volga on school holidays?" He suddenly grows mellow. "Summer evenings on the Zhigali Hills," he continues, "with the colored ships' lights reflected in the water, the echo of the steamers from behind the hills, the sound of a solitary mouth organ from the bows of the nearest boat—yeah." He flips over on his back, stretches, and goes on reminiscing.

I have stopped listening. Wolff has opened my own door to those days. I see, hear, and feel the vivid world of adolescence as if I were in it now.

"And the summer holidays on your estate," I blurt out loudly, "the mad gallops through the steppe, the lazy punting on the brown pond behind your orchard, and the magic nights in your *bashtan*, your melon field, when we helped the watchman pass the time by having him tell us Russian fairy tales . . . ."

"Yeah, that world itself seems like a fairy tale now, a Mennonite fairy tale," Wolff murmurs, gazing up at the rough ceiling.

I get up and in the dim light of the oil lamp rummage around in my chest.

"Here, the only one left from those days," I pass him a ragged photo.

He raises himself and hitches closer to the lamp. "Yeah, that's our young Sasha all right!" He looks amused. "Smart school uniform, optimistic face, confident eyes, the very epitome of Mennonite hopes for the future—just before the Fall. Too bad . . . ."

I look at my youthful image through Wolff's eyes. He's right, of course. I'm standing proudly erect between my parents. My mother looks work-worn but complacent. My father looks strong and self-satisfied. How hard they had worked to acquire our large farm. Bit by bit they had managed to assemble their shared dream. It was not for themselves but for me, their first-born, that they did all this. Serenely ignoring all the portentous signs of national disaster—an ill-fated war with Japan, civil unrest, cries for revolution everywhere, acts of violence, a callously stupid government—they went about their God-ordained business of building a family dynasty that would prosper and endure indefinitely. That was their pious intention.

Will Wolff ask me what happened to my parents? I am tense as I anticipate the question, but he hands back the snapshot without further comment. I put it back with the one of Liese that I showed Wolff when I told him about her shortly after our arrival here.

I lie back in my bunk determined to shut off all further thoughts about Liese, even about myself.

As summer begins to shade into a brief northern autumn, our desperate situation begins to ease somewhat. Food packages arrive from Germany regularly now. Sometimes we even receive gifts of money. The addresses of donors are passed from hand to hand, and most of the begging letters appear to be successful. The packages usually weigh between five and ten kilograms and contain such staples as flour, rice, sugar, and bacon. Almost without exception, they arrive punctually, that is, about two weeks after mailing, and they are released to us promptly and intact. Comma no longer inquires about their origin and purpose. The shipments frequently include reply cards on which the recipients enter their names and the date of reception. From all this we conclude there has been a change in Russian policy and that the entire procedure is approved and supported by the state.

Our morale goes up again. There is a new spirit in the camp. If the packages keep coming, we'll be able to keep going indefinitely. They are an essential shelter against the coming winter, although such a flimsy shelter could blow away at any time. With infinite care we conserve every grain and crumb we receive in order to make the packages go as far as possible. Those who are ailing believe they are recovering faster thanks to the additional nourishment. We workers are convinced that it is revitalizing our bodies.

The northern spring arrives tardily but boldly; the northern fall steals in prematurely and unobtrusively. Only the deciduous trees change color— mainly birches, oaks, and mountain ashes which are in the minority here and hardly noticeable among the masses of green and brown conifers. Too soon the sombre autumn colors will be covered by a layer of white—the most dominant of all northern colors. We'll also be buried here for our second winter.

Our barrack is no longer adequate; we'll have to renovate it before winter sets in. Penner is charged with the responsibility of doing this work. On our next rest day he calls on Koehn and me to help him. We go to the nearby saw-mill and get half a dozen large pine trunks sawn into rough boards. We use some of them to patch the gaping cracks in the walls and roof. We use the rest to lay a floor against the cold and to provide some protection against insects. For almost a year now we've carried on a desperate struggle against fleas and lice and mosquitoes; yet none of us realized until now what a help a floor would be.

In the company of one or two close friends the taciturn Penner sometimes opens up a little. He has a soft, deep voice, and on those rare occasions when he feels like talking he likes to begin with an apt quotation from his beloved Fritz Reuter.

"Dat senn op Stunds sehr schlechte Tiden" (Once in a while these are very difficult times), he quotes drily to Koehn and me as we work on the floor. "Tell me, do you really believe we'll get through another winter here?"

"I believe both, Penner," I answer promptly—"in the wisdom of Fritz Reuter and in our survival this winter. We've got to. We certainly won't be sent south for the winter. In the end—"

"—Yeah," he cuts me off. "I've done a lot of thinking during our time here." He is speaking slowly and deliberately. "At first I thought all this was probably a special measure taken against us Mennonites because of our former economic prosperity and our German culture."

"And now?"

Koehn interrupts. "Now even Penner can see all this is an example of Asiatic cunning, a deliberate war against a whole people, and it makes no difference at all what one is or what it is called."

Penner is still ruminating in his methodical way. "When a man's head has been torn off, you don't grieve over his neck," he quotes the Russian proverb morosely, and drives a nail viciously into the floor.

"By the way," Koehn says, "I was talking to a guy from Number 509 yesterday—it's a Russian camp. He told me he's one of the few inmates there still on his feet. They've got everything there—typhus, scabies, T.B., malnutrition—everywhere sick bodies lying about suffering unattended. They're not even being taken to hospital anymore." He stops and spits to show his disgust. "Of course, we're not so far from that sort of thing either, but at least we haven't reached that stage yet. Just to know that is some comfort, I suppose."

We go back to our sawing and hammering.

But Penner is not satisfied. "Where the Russians are today that's where we Mennonites will be tomorrow, is that what you're saying?"

Koehn is gentler now. "Well, Vasya, maybe it's better not to think in racial terms anymore."

Penner ignores the advice. "So you think we Germans are finished in Russia?"

Koehn spells it out carefully. "I mean that fourteen years of systematic destruction of individuals has thrown the various ethnic groups into such disarray that they are disappearing along with the people. When the state decided to exterminate large numbers of individuals it also sealed the fate of various ethnic groups. We Mennonites will never rise again as a people—unless our children do. But that'll have to happen quickly or it'll be too late."

"*Eck verstoh neuscht mehr*, I can't make sense of it all anymore," Penner says in despair.

Tielmann has received a cheque for twenty marks from abroad. He tells us that he is keeping the money locked away in his chest for a rainy day. We are on our way to work.

"Every day is a rainy day here," Wolff grunts.

"So the idealist has turned capitalist," I joke.

"That's interest, not capital," says Neufeld. "Somebody who has seen our lumber in Germany is trying to salve his conscience. Some business that is." He's on his favorite theme again.

That evening we find the barrack in another uproar. Comma and three of his men came and without uttering a word broke open Tielmann's chest. They took the twenty marks with the warning that from now on all cash is to be turned over to Comma. Apparently it's a new order. No inmate is allowed to keep cash.

How did they know?

Wolff does not mince words. "Tielmann, it was calculated. They knew! Watch it fellows, there's a Judas in our midst."

We stare at each other in consternation. It couldn't possibly be one of us. None of us would do such a thing. Inform to Comma? Never!

Camp Number 513 is honored by a visit from an official delegation. The group consists of political and academic dignitaries, including the writer

Maxim Gorky.[1] We forest workers hear about the visit after the fact.

While we are at work all the barracks are ordered to be cleansed immediately. The floors are carefully sprinkled with greenery and the paths in front of the doors are swept thoroughly. Mothers are ordered to take their children to the nursery promptly; double rations are to be issued there today. The women, along with all walking convalescents, are to report to the administrative office.

Mrs. Penner, who had gone into the forest in the morning to gather and pile firewood and so knew nothing about the visit, happens to return by the back way just as the tour reaches the front of our barrack. She has the sense to stay out of sight, and overhears what Comma, as the proud and informative guide, has to tell the group.

"Gentlemen, I draw your attention to the fact"—his voice is unctuous and self-assured—"that while these buildings have been here for awhile, this settlement was founded only very recently. The settlers arrived here just six weeks ago . . . . Now here we have a typical barrack." Comma indicates the interior of Number 7 with a flourish. He smooths the greenery with his foot while the dignitaries gather around, politely inquisitive, approval already on their faces like an official stamp.

"You can see the floors are sprinkled with greenery daily. There are the simple, sturdy bunks with their occupant's belongings underneath. Now these people are still in a position to supplement their quite adequate official food allotments with the provisions they brought with them. They're all at work right now, and the children are at the nursery school, where they've got it real cozy."

"And the working hours?" one of the guests inquires.

"Our people work between five and seven hours a day," Comma answers smoothly. "As you can appreciate, this far north the conditions are not conducive to long working hours. As far as clothing is concerned, we have met them more than half way, for which they are quite grateful."

"Very good," someone murmurs.

The visitors pass on.

The first snow arrives in late September. The same day Comma invokes another new regulation by ordering everybody who can walk to work in the forest. Even the wives and mothers are obliged to go after taking their children to the nursery for the day. Ohm Peters and Mrs. Preuss are the only ones among us who are declared unfit for work. But according to the same new regulation they are excluded from the rations list completely. We give them their former allotments from our own rations.

There is one other person who is affected by the new regulations, but without apparently suffering any disadvantage. That person is Theresa Preuss, who has been given a job as secretary at the Command Post. I recall

[1]Gorky actually did visit the northern camps in June, 1929, according to Solzhenitsyn's bitter account in *Gulag Archipelago* II, pp. 60-63.

the many walks she took over there during her convalescence in summer. She must have made an impression on somebody.

As usual, Wolff, when aroused, gets to the point bluntly. "So, the Judas in our midst turns out to wear a skirt. Watch it fellows, I smell scandal brewing."

At work, Wolff delicately opens the subject to Martha Preuss. "Well, Marfa Petrovna, how do you feel now that your sex has been given a certain legal status by the new regulations."

Martha blushes, but she meets him head on. "You can speak quite openly, Vladimir Ivanovitch. I know what's on your mind."

Wolff is toying with a pine twig. He hacks it in pieces with precise little strokes.

"All right, so she wants to survive—fine. But she is deceiving herself if she thinks she can postpone her fate indefinitely that way. It'll boomerang on her. Don't forget to tell her that as far as Comma is con—"

"You know that too?"Martha turns away with a stricken look. "Our poor mother!"

Wolff is apologetic. He wants to offer sympathy and moral support, but he is not used to speaking direct words of comfort. He resorts to his usual form of ironic analogy.

"Yes, Marfa Petrovna, we are all, so to speak, attending a difficult school here in order to master a very special subject. We still haven't mastered it, but of course we have a little time left before the final examination."

Wolff slams his axe heavily into the thick oak beside him. "And you know, the funny thing is that the whole exam consists of only two questions: What have you got left? And what are you? *C'est tout!*" His laugh is bitter. "You realize, of course, we are still only facing the first question. When our existence here—after the loss of our former prosperity and social status—has torn the last shred of self-respect out of us then, and only then, will we arrive at the second question. When we finally understand the implications of that question we won't want to answer it. What will we say? 'A *former* man of honor, and *ex*-truthful person, a *once*-decent human being?' No, my dear . . . we won't even want to admit that we are Mennonites, or claim any status or identity for ourselves at all. The only proper and permissible answer to the question will consist of just one word. That word will turn out to have been the real subject of our studies here. It will sum up the ultimate meaning of all this painful nonsense. The word is *'Nothing'—nothing at all!* Do you follow me?"

He stops, suddenly self-conscious of his own passionate rhetoric. He grins down at the girl apologetically, his eyes intense.

Martha, large dark eyes full of pain, says nothing, but she has deciphered the secret message of love encoded in Wolff's speech.

Walking beside Martha on the way home, he returns to the subject of Theresa. "Don't berate your sister for her—betrayal. Comfort her by pointing out that all of us are forced into betrayal daily here—against the ideals of our people, who have already receded into nothing but a memory for us—against humanity itself, which now exists for us only in books read a long time ago."

We find Theresa in the barrack visiting her mother. Without a trace of embarrassment she explains to Martha that her new job as secretary in Coma's office requires her to live with the other female personnel at the Command Post. She has come to fetch her things but promises to come for visits as often as possible. Martha's face is pale and expressionless. Neither girl is able to look directly at her mother. Theresa strokes her mother's hand and promises to bring her a special treat on her next visit.

Theresa's place in the barrack is taken by a widow from the Crimea and her three children, who range in age from three or four to about ten. Mrs. Zimmermann is a handsome woman in her early thirties. There is an air of refinement about her cruelly out of place in these surroundings. She reminds me with a pang of my Liese—the round, full brow, the finely etched eyebrows, the way she delicately cocks her head on the graceful stalk of her neck. Her hair, a beautiful auburn, is neatly coiled around her shapely head. A fine-looking woman.

The boy of ten has an open, intelligent face which soon draws me into conversation with him.

"Well, my friend, and what's your name?"

"Erwin Zimmermann."

"So, you're a carpenter then?"

He laughs self-consciously at my little joke.

"You look as though you've done your share of traveling, Erwin."

He looks at me warily, then over at his mother, who nods encouragement. "Yes, quite a lot, I guess."

"And lived in various places?"

"Oh yes," he is beginning to relax a little. "In Novorossiisk, in Kharkov, Feodosiya, Melitopol, and here."

He pronounces the names in a flawless Russian accent. Poor lad! In his short decade he has already been forced to roam through most of southern Russia. No wonder he is wary of strangers.

"That's quite a list. And when did you start on this latest journey?"

Again the suspicious look. The youthful eyes betray the same fear that has plagued us all for so many years now, the fear of saying too much to a friendly neighbor.

"You can tell me Erwin. Look, I'm German too."

His gaze slips to the floor. "Yeah, but those others were German too—"

"Who?"

"The men who helped shoot Papa and—" he stops in confusion and again looks for guidance from his mother. She nods encouragement. "You can tell the gentleman about that."

Erwin runs his eyes over me critically. "Mama, he's not a gentleman!"

"Erwin—!" Mrs. Zimmermann is embarrassed.

I laugh boisterously. "And why am I not a gentleman?"

The boy blushes. "Gentlemen," he stammers, "wear a nice suit —and, and look neat—and—." Words fail him. "Papa was a gentleman," he adds, visibly relieved to be able to provide an example at least.

"And what did your papa look like?"

He has found his bearings again. "I can show you—like this—." He fetches a photo out of his mother's pocket.

"Please!" Mrs. Zimmermann nods amiably at me. "He's very proud of his father."

The face in the photo is that of a clever, self-aware man, strong with the confidence and pride of his class. I study the picture closely. The boy certainly resembles his father, who represents a human type which has disappeared from Russia as though plucked away by some giant's hand. It is a face which belongs to pre-Revolutionary Russia. It represents a bourgeois class which has been purged from the land so completely that it is hard to believe it ever existed. Zimmermann's face looks as obsolete as that of Tsar Nicholas II.

"Yes," Erwin says with dignity, "that was Papa."

Mrs. Zimmermann, who is as charming as her son, fills in the details. Her husband had been somewhat older than she. At the time of their marriage in 1918 he was the managing director of a brewery in the Siberian city of Tomsk. He lost his position as a result of the Civil War and took refuge with his young wife, who was pregnant with their first child, in his native city of Novorossiisk in the Caucasus. There her husband found employment for a time with a firm that had not yet been nationalized. In the meantime they had lost their first child at birth. From Novorossiisk they retreated northwards to the Ukrainian city of Kharkov, where Erwin was born.

Branded a *burzhui,* her husband found it ever more difficult to find employment. Finally, he secured a modest position as bookkeeper in a state enterprise at Feodosiya in the Crimea. There they lived several years in humble but peaceful circumstances. Then one day two German-speaking GPU men came to the town, spoke to various German neighbors, and proceeded to her husband's office. They told her later that they shot her husband for trying to escape custody. Forced to leave Feodosiya, Mrs. Zimmermann went with her three children to live in Melitopol with her husband's sister until her own arrest several months ago.

The woman tells her story simply and with few emotional overtones. It is a matter-of-fact summary which she has probably swapped many times for similar stories from other exiles with whom she has traveled. The main outlines of these stories have a frightening similarity: only the details differ. I observe her covertly as she talks. She has a habit of pausing slightly to emphasize certain words, and to raise the curve of one eyebrow when she mentions a significant detail. Her voice is a rich contralto—again so much like—."

"But I must be boring you, dear sir—," she breaks off with a blush.

"No, no, dear lady, in this country we never tire of hearing each other's life stories." I turn to the boy again. "So, I'm not a gentleman, Erwin." I try to lighten the mood.

He shakes his head, but he is embarrassed now. Suddenly I feel ashamed for myself. I murmur an excuse and leave the barrack.

I wander down our work-trail until I am lost in the trees. I stop and sit down on an old black stump. My conversation with Mrs. Zimmermann and her son has left me strangely disturbed. Both of them revive personal memories I have been successful in suppressing of late. I examine myself. The boy is right, of course. Whatever marks of middle-class gentility I had have long since disappeared from my person. Outwardly I look like a beggar; inwardly I have become hard and unfeeling.

But there is something else that bothers me far more—the realization that if Liese and our son had lived they would be about the same age as Mrs. Zimmermann and Erwin. Oh, my lost love, my darling girl. Would my life be any better now if you had lived? To think of you and our son in a place like this is unbearable. The brief savagery of your end spared you so much protracted, piecemeal suffering and degradation. You could not possibly have grown the tough hide required for survival here. Nor has Mrs. Zimmermann, I suspect. And what about me? Condemned to die, I survive here only because the better part of me died long ago. No, Liese, I could not wish you in Mrs. Zimmermann's place.

Several days later, during the noon dinner break, an ugly quarrel takes place between Martha and Theresa, who has brought her mother some special foodstuffs such as we have not seen for a long time.

"Theresa, how could you?" Martha whispers harshly as she accompanies her sister to the door.

Theresa does not bother to keep her voice down. "What did you expect me to do? I wasn't strong enough to work in the forest anymore, and—and I was tired of going hungry." She turns and glares at the rest of us. "Believe me, I was desperate. Wait'll you reach that point."

She turns back to the door and addresses Martha again, pleading now. "Martha, you know this arrangement makes it easier for Mother—the extra food. And if you want—".

Martha angrily grabs the girl by the shoulders and shakes her roughly. "Theresa, have you gone crazy? Have you forgotten everything— Father—family honor—your honor? My own sister—with that—phui—!"

"Martha, shut up!" Theresa screams, and tries to wrench herself free of her sister's grasp.

But the outraged Martha is past caring now. All her pent-up shame and rage over her sister's behavior come spilling out in a stream of recrimination. "All these horrible years we've lived and suffered together—the three of us—now you—you go to that filth—you slut—mistress of a *commissar*!"

It's out now. For a moment there is shocked silence.

"Martha!" Wild-eyed, Theresa storms out of the barrack, pursued by the accusing voice of her enraged sister. "And the twenty marks are on your conscience too, you traitoress!"

Mrs. Preuss, the pastor's widow, lies cowering and weaping on her bunk.

After that we do not see Theresa in the barrack again. She comes back a few times with food for her mother, but only when the rest of us are at work.

Parcels are again arriving from Germany. Their arrival marks the rare days when it is still possible to see happy faces in camp. One can count the number of shipments that have just arrived by those faces. For a few hours the impassive features and dull eyes brighten. Men who greeted their sentence of "loss of state rights" with stony silence get tears in their eyes when they receive a new winter jacket. Women who once lived in the midst of abundance weep with joy over a five-kilogram package containing a few foodstuffs. Children wasted with hunger dance around the little box begging gleefully.

"You know," Wolff philosophizes from his bunk, "those are our feast days; we get them as a kind of compensation here."

"So your chronic pessimism turns out to be unjustified," I chaff him. "It's still possible to feel a little joy in this world, even if it's only over a few grains of rice."

"*Touché, touché,* oh voice of conscience,"Wolff concedes with a bleak smile. Then his face tightens. "But do you want to know what evil thoughts come to me over this?"

"Naturally, even here you would find a hair in the soup," I retort sharply.

But he ignores me. "I'm convinced that an organization exists over there—perhaps several—and that it has become a kind of occupational thing to send us packages. The people over there live their lives planning, earning, spending. The little compassion they have left for us they put neatly into a little box and mail it to us. And then come the heartwarming statistics which affluent business directors check over before driving in their big cars to the dazzling delights of theatres and nightclubs—"

"—Wolff stop it!"

He props himself up on one elbow and looks at me intently.

"My hunger is private and—to me, at least—sacred, Sasha. It's with me night and day; it's the voice in my belly that pleads with me to go on living just a little longer. It gives me the only identity I have left: I hunger therefore I am . . . ." His voice drops to a cold whisper. "I resent my hunger being exploited, becoming the basis of a lucrative business enterprise."

"My God, Volodya! How can you—?"

Wolff continues to glare at me, then abruptly turns his back.

Our second winter brings us another gift, the dreaded hunger typhus. The victims are suddenly overcome with alternate hot and cold fits. Hour-long spells of the cold shivers are followed by terrible sweating spells. Along with sharp, stabbing pains in their extremities, the patients are plagued by endless vomiting. Their weakened constitutions offer little resistance to the disease.

The onslaught of typhus quickly destroys the cautious spirit of optimism we had built up in the fall. Once again a terrible apathy hangs over Camp 513. In Number Seven we watch listlessly, almost indifferently, as first Penner and then Mrs. Preuss and Hans Neufeld are carted off to Andreievka. Comma is compelled to order daily transports to the hospital. Blustering as always he threatens to let the whole camp die off if the demand for transportation gets any worse.

The typhus victims are taken away and no one seems to care. Even their relatives seem to accept their illness with almost sub-human indifference. Theresa Preuss no longer comes near our barrack and perhaps doesn't even know that her mother has been stricken. When the surviving patients return to us weeks later looking more dead than alive we greet them matter-of-factly, without showing much interest. Everything is accepted as routine here.

The news of Penner's death reaches us early one morning just as we are preparing to go to work. Mrs. Penner, weeping piteously as she hugs her un-comprehending son, begs us over and over to fetch her husband's body from the hospital so that "he won't be thrown into a common pit," as she puts it. Nobody seems to know just when or under what circumstances the poor chap's secluded life came to an end.

Ohm Peters, tearfully supported by the widow, wants to give Penner a proper burial. Considering the nervous state the administration is in over the epidemic, we deem it a risky business at best. But we respect the old man's indomitable sense of duty, and we would all like to pay our last respects to our old village carpenter who is the first of our villagers to die here.

We discover that corpses are left in a crude morgue—just an old shed really—until the third day. If no one has claimed them they are buried somewhere in a mass grave, the "pit" that so terrifies Mrs. Penner. We go to claim Penner's body on the second day. We have brought spades and other tools. Wolff has taken his axe. "It's a woodcutter's kind of work," he explains.

We look around for a suitable cemetery; we know there will be more occasions of this kind. Not far from Andreievka, on the edge of the forest, there is a magnificent grove of birches which seems appropriate for our purposes. No timber is being cut there yet.

The ground is already frozen solid; in fact, the frost goes down a good meter. We begin to hack out a grave; at the meter and a half level our strength is gone. We decide in this iron soil that is a deep enough hole.

We carry Penner's body to the grave on a light plank bier. His wife has removed his jacket and shoes. She'll be needing them herself now.

Above the bushy black beard, the dead man's sharp white face is starkly upturned to the tree tops. Oddly enough, it looks more open now, less inscrutable than it did in life.

Ohm Peters shakily turns the pages of his Bible. He looks almost as white as Penner. The old man is so feeble that he will be forced to keep it very short, I surmise. But he surprises me.

". . . by your rejoicing which I have in Christ Jesus our Lord, I die daily," he reads in his thin voice.

He clears his throat and looks up.

"Our departed brother knew the bitter truth of those words. We are all living under a daily sentence of physical death here," he gestures in the direction of the Camp. "There is no need for me to preach about that.

"But there is another form of dying, according to the Apostle, that is even more bitter than physical death. And that is," he searches for the right words. "And that is a death in which a man, of his own free will, renounces this life within himself. Doing that is to suffer an inner death very different from the one we all must suffer here below."

Ohm Peters shuts his Bible and puts it in his side pocket. "And this inner death in conjunction with Christ now becomes another life, a freshly granted life." His voice falters and catches in a spasm of dry coughing. "This death is a rejoicing," he wheezes, "whereas there is nothing to rejoice in the other kind of death.

"Our brother Penner has now experienced both forms of death. He was a quiet man but his spirit ran deep. He suffered along with the rest of us, and now has been delivered from this harsh world. But he had experienced Paul's inner death long before; and that life through death is now his glory."

He pauses and looks at each of us in turn. "Who can say which of us will be the next to be laid in this frozen ground? But if we have already died to the Lord then, like William Penner, we will not have died in vain even here in the North."

The reedy voice falls silent for a few moments. Then it rises again in a calm, simple prayer, as we stand there bare-headed, fur caps in hand. The sun reflects a few pallid rays against the speckled birch trunks. We summon all our remaining energy to heave the hard clods back into the grave.

As we start for home I can't help wondering whether Penner would have been able to provide an apt quotation from Fritz Reuter for an occasion such as this.

Wolff and I are hacking at the trunk of a mountain ash. With typical offhandedness he confides a secret to me. "Well, old man, I'm afraid I'll have to render you speechless again."

"You've received notice of another parcel?"

"Can't you think of anything else? No, this has nothing to do with any parcel. You know, Sasha, even here by the White Sea it's not good for a person to be alone."

I begin to doubt Wolff's sanity. "So your own misery isn't enough for you, Volodya. You want to take on a double share?"

"No, just to balance the misery a little. There'll still be the same amount for each of us."

"The same amount? You've gone stir-crazy, my friend. It's funerals we observe here, not weddings. Don't you realize that?"

Wolff laughs ruefully, loosens his muffler and moves over to my side. "I'll admit you're right, in one sense. In another sense, though, I see life sliding by,

Sasha. For what purpose are we struggling to survive? What's it all for? In the past people like you and me served our people in whatever capacity we could, but all that is past. Now half of them are gone . . . and the other half will be drowned too in a little while. I tell you Sasha, it's all come to nothing. We're all lost!

"This is our second winter here—maybe there'll be a third. I can't bear to face it alone. I need the warmth and love of another human being to share the terrible void, to soothe the weariness in my soul. Alone, I just can't take this life any longer. I'll accept every bit of comfort I can find—a piece of bread, warmer boots, a wife! Maybe it is all part of the death struggle—or madness as you say."

He sits down heavily on a trunk. "You know, Sasha, sometimes in the evenings I'd just like to run out into the snow and howl like the wolf I am. But I don't. I talk and joke and laugh and pretend that I'm still sane. I cling to life and act as though it still means something when I know it doesn't. I persuade myself we can follow a normal routine here—work for our daily bread, have social intercourse, and even maintain some semblance of spiritual life. It's all different from before, of course, but it's all here. The dying is here too, different from before. And if death why not marriage, different from before? That's part of the pattern too."

Wolff gives a grim laugh and bends towards me. "Look, old friend, life is still the same, it's just that it is taking place at a lower level—"

"—of hell, Volodya!"

"Of hell. All right, it's the level of a frozen hell, if you like. But even in hell one desires to live."

I can't bear to hear him go on this way. I extend my hand. "Volodya, it's all right, I understand—*s bogom*, go with God!"

He grasps my hand eagerly. "*S bogom*, he repeats, "that has a warm sound. Thanks, Sasha. I appreciate that."

"I'll wish Marfa Petrovna the same this evening, Volodya."

The typhus is thinning out our ranks. While Mrs. Preuss and Hans Neufeld are gradually recuperating, Koehn's older daughter gets sick. Then tiny, self-effacing Mrs. Albrecht comes down with typhus. Two days later she dies in hospital.

Ohm Peters, her father, bears his grief stoically. "She has been delivered," he says simply. "I too yearn for release."

We bury Mrs. Albrecht in the birch grove beside Penner. We place a small wooden cross on the raw, stiff mound. Her name and date of death have been carved in the cross with a pocket knife.

This time the old man is even briefer. His words, sharp and clear, come straight from his serenely accepting heart. He sounds utterly sincere when he says he is thankful for his daughter's death. His small grandson stands beside him looking thin and subdued.

My mind is made up at last. One morning I call Wolff and Koehn over to one side. I feel awkward telling them. "Wolff has told us his secret—" I look from one to the other—" now I want to tell you mine."

"Not Anna Zimmermann, old buddy?" Wolff looks shocked.

I glare at him.

"What's up now?" Koehn demands perplexed.

I don't know how to say it. "I—I want to get away from here."

They exchange startled glances. Snow crunches underfoot. Wolff draws up his shoulders and tugs at his belt.

"You want to get away? Now who's crazy? You'd only be exchanging one prison for another one much worse, man."

Koehn has a stunned, hang-dog look.

I point to the west.

"Well, and how?"

"First to Apostleart. From there I'll take it as it comes."

"That's insane." Koehn comes to life. "Let the two guys in 508 tell you how miserably things went for them when they tried it. They were lucky to make it back here. Their buddy landed in the concentration camp at Archangel."

"I've talked to them."

He shakes his head, pleading. "Don't try it Sasha. You'll never make it."

"Look, I just can't go on here, it's as simple as that. I'm not risking anything, really. I've got nothing to lose, except you two."

Wolff surprises me. "That's right," he agrees, as though he hadn't heard my last words. "In the end it'll be a good thing for us, assuming you'll make it, to have our own propagandist out there."

I stare at him. Is he being facetious even now?

"*S bogom!* Sasha." He claps me on the shoulders vigorously. "But keep your head, especially in spring."

"In spring? No, no Volodya, by spring I intend to be long gone from these mushy swamps. It's got to be now, in winter. At least I'll have solid footing."

Wolff shows alarm. "But not before New Year's! You promised to be my best man. The look he gives me is a plea I can't resist.

"*Khorosho,* after New Year's."

Koehn has jammed his hands deep into his pockets and stares out to the west. He makes no further attempt to dissuade me.

The work in the forest is getting steadily more difficult. Or perhaps it just seems that way because we are getting weaker. We start at seven in the morning now. During the two-hour noon break we march the three kilometers back to Camp. It is a half hour walk. Then we take turns standing in line at the camp kitchen for up to three-quarters of an hour. That gives us only fifteen to twenty minutes to eat our dinner before the half-hour walk back to work. We work until around ten at night and many days we do not get back to Camp much before eleven. The depressing fact is that while the work norms have not been increased our capacity for work has decreased.

Relief comes just in time. Beginning in November we get a rest day every sixth day. Incomprehensible as it seems, we are even granted an increase in our bread ration. The forest workers now receive 750 grams daily—"so that the misery can stretch out a little longer," according to Neufeld.

Without prior notification I receive a short fur jacket from home, and again I suffer less from the cold. But my good fortune doesn't even last until Christmas. I am obliged to barter it in the villages for buckwheat groats.

Then a terrible thing happens to Koehn, who takes over the wearying business of bartering. One morning he sets out for the villages with his son Willy. Four days later Koehn returns empty-handed, sick and heartbroken. Willy is not with him.

Apparently Koehn and Willy had gone through the various settlements nearby, but had found nothing to barter for. They were forced to go farther afield. When they got to Ustjug they decided to try and hitch a ride on some transport or other. They were just in time to catch a lumber train which was starting to move out. Koehn was able to swing aboard the last car easily, but the youngster panicked when he clutched the frozen metal with his bare hands. He lost his hold, fell under the wheels, and was instantly killed. The distraught father then ran around trying to get some assistance in burying the mangled remains of his son. He finally got two young men in Ustjug to help him, but it cost him the bartering goods he had with him.

There is a deep pall of gloom over the barrack as the Koehn family mourns Willy, who was a cheerful, likeable lad much like his father. Koehn himself is inconsolable. His health seems broken and he becomes unrecognizable. At night he often falls into delirium and raves about the fatal accident and about camp life in general. The coming of day finds him pale and shaken and so weak he can't get out of bed.

"I guess Koehn is getting ready to pack his bags too," Neufeld mutters one morning. "Poor bastard." A surprising show of sympathy, coming from Neufeld.

But Koehn pulls through. Two weeks later he is back at work with us, shaky but determined. Maria Koehn has also taken the death of her oldest child hard, but she has the good sense not to blame her husband for the accident.

Attempts at escape are growing more frequent, but the administration shows no signs of panic. Comma knows exactly what measures to take. He offers food bounties for escaped prisoners in the surrounding villages and camps. Anybody who kills an escapee is rewarded with thirty-five to forty-five kilograms of rye flour when he brings in the corpse. For a live one he gets up to ninety kilograms. The system is effective. The impoverished small-farmers in the area welcome the extra income. So far we know of no escapees who have made it through to freedom. We hear that even some of the exiles have offered Comma their services in reporting or recapturing escapees.

Late one evening Neufeld brings in a sack of flour. Hoping we are all asleep, he tries to sneak it under his bunk. But several of us are still awake and watch him from our bunks.

"Well, comrade Neufeld," Wolff says grimly. "Traded your last good shirt?" No answer from Neufeld. "Or your soul?"

"Yeah, my soul!" he snarls, angry at having been exposed. "My precious soul, yeah." He laughs derisively. "We'll see how long you'll be able to live with yours, you smug bastards."

"Hans," Koehn says with quiet compassion, "it probably requires more than good intentions and a respectable past to remain upright here. But there is finally a limit—"

"—before we're all buried here at the North Pole."

Wolff is now thoroughly aroused. "So we shove each other a little to speed up the slow slide to hell, eh dear countryman? You seem to be of the opinion that a little more dirty business before we are all buried under the birches won't make much difference. And it doesn't even matter if it's done against one's own blood, does it?" Wolff has worked himself into such a rage that the whole barrack has been aroused. "But if you've chosen the role of Judas in our little drama don't forget the rope, that's part of it too. Don't forget that! But apparently you—" he stops in mid-sentence, lifts up the sack, and hurls it against Neufeld's bunk with a force that makes the flour dust puff up in a cloud—"you still plan to live with us for awhile yet." He stops breathless, glaring murderously at Neufeld.

Neufeld doesn't answer. He kicks off his boots and stretches out on his bunk without touching his sack again.

Wolff and Martha had intended to celebrate their "Arctic wedding", as he calls it, at Christmas time. But they have bad luck. Early in December it begins to snow as if heaven in its mercy had decided to bury us all softly in white. In the weeks that follow, our clothes get so soaked on the job that one after the other of us comes down with a bad cold. Wolff's "snow bride" develops a violent cough accompanied by a fever. By December twenty-third she is coughing blood, and Wolff is trying desperately to find her some medicine. He appeals to Theresa, but in vain. All Theresa can offer her sister is some extra bread, which the sick girl rejects indignantly. She would rather die than accept any help from that "camp girl" she says. Finally Wolff sees no other way than to take his bride to the hospital in Andreievka, even though he does not trust the facilities or care in the place.

At work Wolff is despondent and pessimistic, although he avoids speaking directly about his fears for Martha. "It's hard to bear, Sasha. A year in the North seems to have a greater effect on you than a lifetime elsewhere. It's like centrifugal force in physics," he prescribes a circle with his fist. "The stronger the whirling movement from Moscow, the more our lives here by the polar sea disintegrate and reduce themselves to helpless atoms. We are splitting apart here. Our bodies and spirits are at the mercy of forces over which we have no control, man. It's frightening." He gestures forlornly. "There's no use beating around the bush, Sasha, we're finished—*kaput*, miserably and helplessly lost." He looks up at me with an expression that tears my heart. "So, you have a yen to travel?"

"Yes, Volodya, very soon, especially under these miserable conditions."

"I envy you," he says simply; "at any other time I would have gone with you, but—" he points back in the direction of the Camp," I have Martha. As soon as she's well enough we'll get married and share our lot as long as we can."

His eyes brighten and his voice sounds urgent. "If you do make it," he brings his fist down on my shoulder so hard I stagger, "you must raise a real storm, a public storm that will make the whole world know what is happening here. Tell them we're squirming in the bloody jaws of a monster such as the world has never seen before. Maybe even then it'll be too late, maybe you'll just be delivering a funeral oration over us, but tell them anyhow. Tell them our hell may be frozen but our suffering burns like fire. Ask them to examine their imported lumber for our bloody fingerprints."

Wolff is actually shedding tears. I have never seen him so deeply moved. "We thought we knew how to live; that part was easy," his voice has sunk to a hollow whisper. "But now we are learning to die, slowly, by inches . . . and . . . that . . . that . . . that . . . is much . . . harder, Sasha."

For a long time I debate privately whether I should say goodbye to the others or disappear without notice. I decide on the latter, much as it pains me not to tell them. It's not that I don't trust them, even Neufeld; it's myself I am worried about. My powers of resistence are too low. Every look, handclasp, or dissuading word would shake my resolve to go through with my escape.

Two days before my planned attempt I plead illness and remain behind in the barrack. I tie up in a sack the small supply of bread I have been hoarding and hide it carefully. I calculate I have enough for three or four days. Then I try to go back to sleep. I want to store up as much energy as I can. I know I cannot risk sleeping as long as I'm in the forest. Sleeping outside in the winter here means certain death.

The camp guard who checks the barrack in the mornings takes me for sick and doesn't bother me. I doze fitfully, awaking from time to time with a start. And then I begin sweating with the same doubts. Have I got the nerve? Is my timing right? Will I find food and shelter in time? And what about those I leave behind? Will there be reprisals against them? I have asked Wolff and he doesn't think so. He has also convinced me that I have an obligation to try and smuggle our hideous story out to the world. I know how slim my chances are, but I can't bear to stay here any longer! I fall asleep again.

I do the same the second day.

That night, New Year's Eve, I wait until I am sure everybody is asleep and then quietly steal out of barrack Number Seven. As I pass by Wolff's bunk he reaches out and squeezes my arm.

I head west, directly for the Finnish border. The weather is clear and not too cold. I check my little thermometer and find it reads minus twenty-five. Where the trees are sparse I can see the stars; although they are not as bright as the northern lights. I can identify individual constellations quite clearly.

Thank God for the bright northern night! The glittering snow helps me find a path through the trees with less difficulty than I had anticipated. The snow comes up to my knees and higher and slows my progress. How I long to get out of this accursed forest, even though it protects me from the lung-tearing winter winds of the open tundra. At first the noise of axe-strokes, saws, and breaking trunks still rings in my ears, and I catch myself looking around in alarm more than once. But gradually I become attuned to the primeval silence in these endless wastes of trees and snow. In fact, the silence becomes so permeating that I feel threatened by it. It's as though it is coming at me from all sides, squeezing me into itself slowly and inexorably. My footsteps plunging through the deep snow are merely a puny, ludicrous violation of the awesome stillness all around me.

Dawn at last filters timidly through the pines and birches and sprays the snow unevenly with wan splotches of light. Nothing else changes for awhile. The stars are still there, only paler, and the northern lights play tag as riotously as before. If there are animals or birds here I do not see or hear them. It's eerie to be so alone. I could sink into the forest's icy dreams and disappear without a trace. In the Far North trails and footsteps are reliable only if they reach doors.

After a night of awkward plodding I begin to falter. Although I have halted frequently to rest, I have remained standing each time and have taken only a few minutes to catch my breath. I'm beginning to lose my balance a lot in the deep snow, a sure sign that I'm getting weary. There is no place to sit down, so I lean against a tree, gnaw down a piece of frozen bread, and lick up some snow. Whatever else happens, I won't run out of water to drink. I close my eyes and try to doze standing up, but even though I'm dog-tired I'm too jumpy to relax.

I stiffen as I hear footsteps approaching. Then a man's voice. My God! Comma couldn't possibly have discovered my escape so soon. I hunker down behind the big pine and wait. The sounds are definitely getting closer. How many? If they find my tracks I am dead.

Then a hundred meters away, I see a strange figure staggering through the snow with stiff, awkward motions. Every few steps the man flails his arms aloft, as though fighting off insects. He seems to be in a state of panic. He keeps up a constant guttural chatter broken frequently by wild, hair-raising laughter.

Who is he? Certainly not one of Comma's men. He looks more like an inmate, an escaped prisoner who has lost his way. My blood runs cold. Clearly, the poor creature has lost his mind and is wandering aimlessly in this unpeopled wilderness. I watch him flailing away, looking straight ahead, cursing and laughing.

Feeling selfish and cowardly, I decide not to come out of hiding. How could I help the poor wretch? I need all my strength and nourishment for myself.

I watch the man as he disappears slowly among the trees and then I continue walking in the opposite direction.

For awhile I concentrate on the sounds of my own exertion, but the silence begins to mesmerize me again. Did I really see and hear another human being in this nightmarish landscape? I become uncertain. Was my mind playing tricks? Was it the kind of apparition that comes to people who are suffering from snow madness? I know there is such a thing. I have a giddy sense of having lost track of time; time seems to have dissolved into space. My senses feel disembodied and seem to float away from my struggling figure in the snow. What if time and space have leaped ahead and it was myself I saw lurching blindly through the trees?

I stop to rest again, to get a grip on my badly shaken nerves. My only chance for survival is to husband my energy carefully and remain clear-headed.

Gradually the scenery changes. The trees are smaller and there are more open spaces. I am reaching the edge of the forest. In the clearings the snow has piled towers and walls higher than a man on top of the mounds of moss. I skirt them carefully. A tundra of peat hillocks lies before me, mound upon snow-covered mound. The few dwarf birches growing among them are so drifted over as to be barely visible. Here and there the winds have blown bare patches of ice.

I look back. The forest looms behind me like a huge black wall, a protective wall I now realize. There is a biting, gusty wind in my face which reduces my breathing to shallow, uneven gasps. I try turning my back on it, but it is too difficult to walk backwards in the snow. I am forced to walk sideways, face averted, moving ahead in little lurches, like a swimmer doing the dog-paddle.

The wind quickly wears down my remaining energy. I feel bone-weary and ready to drop. How long is it since I've slept? I've lost track of time. Worse still, I'm no longer sure of my direction because of the cloud cover that has blotted out the sun for many hours now. What if I'm walking north instead of west? I may never reach a settlement at all.

I am seized by panic. My fear of meeting people has given way to the terror of finding myself in a world empty of all life. My vision seems to be out of focus. Is it just the wind filling my eyes? I begin to see fantastic images growing out of the snow. The silent, menacing figures are all around me. Voices howl in the wind. I must keep going. Friends, my story . . . outside world . . . depending on me . . . sleep, for nothing . . . safe in the arms . . . no Liese—better to die right now . . . all for nothing . . . Wolff said better frozen hell . . . must not fail . . . forest, Comma here—get me—warm bunk . . . lie down . . . rest . . ..

My ears register the swish of sleigh runners and guttural voices. I open my eyes. I am lying under a stiff horse blanket. As I move my head slightly I see two dark, huddled backs above me. The voices are Russian. Rifles are propped up in front of them. Are they hunters? Or guards?

They hear me stirring and look down. "Where you from?" the older one asks and surveys me with mild curiosity. "We saw you staggering around the edge of the forst an hour ago. Then we lost you and almost drove over you in the snow."

I am suspicious. I can't discern the marks of his trade on his person. Is he really a hunter?

"Don't you understand Russian?" he begins again. I have nothing to lose. I may as well speak up.

"Of course, I do. Thank you for picking me up. Where are you taking me?"

They ignore my question, but the younger one gives me a look that comes close to being compassionate.

"Yeah."

"How long have you been running?"

"I—I'm not sure. Three days I think."

They accept my answers without further comment, as though inmates on the run are a common occurence. The conversation appears to be over. The older man pulls on the lines to quicken the horse's pace, but the snow is deep and the going laborious. The sleigh climbs up and down the moss hillocks like a boat in choppy waters.

The hours pass. The two men talk hunting mostly. They make no further attempt to question me. Through half-closed lids I observe the passing landscape over the low sideboards of the sleigh. My body feels numb and I wonder if I have any frostbite. I try working my toes in my tattered felt boots but I feel nothing. My fingers are also stiff and numb. I press them deeper into my pockets and pray they aren't frozen. I won't know until I get to a warm place.

At twilight the sleigh stops in front of a wooden hut in a tiny village. "Get down," the driver orders. "We're here."

The hunters turn out to be my saviors in more ways than one. They help relieve the excruciating pain of thawing out my extremities by rubbing them with snow. Together we ascertain the damage to my hands and feet. I do have a touch of frostbite on most of my toes but my hands are just badly chilled. Luckily, there will be no permanent damage, although my feet swell so badly I am unable to put my boots back on that evening.

They give me some dried fish and buckwheat bread and I eat ravenously. After I have eaten and the throbbing in my toes has let up I lie down on the oven bench and sleep around the clock.

The hunters have an amazing knowledge of the region. They provide me with useful information for the rest of my trip, although I don't tell them my exact destination. I decide to risk going on, but after hearing my hosts' description of the whole area I change my destination to Archangel. With their help I draw a rough map showing the larger settlements and how to circumvent them so as to avoid the police. The map also indicates the main features of the terrain in the region.

Next day, my feet still very tender, I set out for Archangel. The villages are more numerous in this arid region than I would have supposed, and I am never in danger of not finding shelter. They are mainly hunting and fishing villages. My ragged appearance seems to arouse sympathy in these primitive people. Although Russian peasants generally are suspicious of strangers, the villagers here are very friendly and generous. They not only give me shelter but share their modest food supplies with me. Dried fish and bread become my staple diet.

Helped by moderate weather and hospitable peasants, I make my way to Archangel in short, relatively easy stages. For better or worse, I reach the city in a little over three weeks.

Like other northern towns and settlements I have seen, Archangel is not exactly a picture of prosperity. The streets look busier than those of Vologda, but there is an air of futility everywhere. The people on the streets (mainly Russians and Zyrians with some Western Europeans and Samoyeds) look shabby and poor. Traditionally, most of the population is engaged in such northern trades as lumber and furs, as well as in the handling of grain from the South. But I see precious few signs of the grain trade. The economic conditions of our country no longer allow for the exporting of that precious commodity.

My appearance doesn't seem to attract any attention. I look like one of the lumberjacks who can be seen here in droves. Nobody looks at me, nobody stops me. For a time I drift around the streets trying to get the feel of the place.

It is not too long before I find my way down to the harbor. Although it does not appear to be very busy, the colorful harbor scene strikes my eyes like an exotic vision from another planet. I stare entranced at the foreign freighters with their fluttering flags which represent beckoning, enticing oases of freedom that offer escape from the northern desert. To my left I see the squat, rust-copper hull of a Danish ship, to the right the longer slimmer twin-masted bulk of a Swedish freighter. There are other ships of all sizes behind them, each with its native crew from a country I have never seen. My heart soars! Here is my passport to freedom.

I walk up the gangplank of the Danish ship without being challenged. Gingerly I open the door of the forward cabin and find myself in the presence of the grey-haired captain. Very politely but firmly, betraying no surprise at my presence, he says no to my murmured request for asylum. He doesn't even seem surprised to hear me speak German. It would be too risky for him, he explains gently, and advises me to try other ships.

Somewhat deflated but by no means discouraged, I walk over to the Swedish ship, its blue-yellow flag bright over its bow. There are huge stacks of lumber on the quay waiting to be loaded. Russian stevedores are just guiding a crane-load of lumber down into the hold. I wait until they disappear and then steal aboard. Again I have no trouble finding the captain's cabin. I give a nervous little knock and wait for the invitation to enter.

"Captain, sir—" I stammer.

He looks up, startled by the unfamiliar voice. "Yes? What do you want?"

He also speaks German. I blurt out at once. "Captain, sir, please help a fleeing German colonist who has suffered a year and a half of terrible exile in the North, and—and before that over a decade of hardship in Soviet Russia. I'm only one of millions. Won't you save me—take me with you—? I'm actually wringing my hands in my eagerness to persuade him.

He is as coolly polite as the Dane, and just as negative. "Forgive me, sir," a slight blush appears on his face, "but that's impossible." He looks down at his papers, then glances at his watch. "You'll have to excuse me; the Russian patrol will be along any minute. They make half-hour checks along the quay and on board ship." He nods in dismissal.

His smooth dismissal angers me. "Sir! You are carrying Russian timber which we exiles have cut with our life's blood. You are doing business with a government which persecutes citizens for the crime of wanting to remain individuals and practising Christians. Can't you see—?" In my rage I bring my fist down sharply on the captain's desk.

He raises his hand in a defensive gesture, then nervously rubs his forehead with a soft white hand as he tries to gauge the threat I present.

My frustration makes me reckless. "Let me tell you something—you, you—"

Before I can finish he grabs his wallet and offers me a Swedish five-kroner note.

"Money?" I roar, beside myself with rage. "You dismiss me with money? With money—money?"

I stumble down the gangplank in a blind fury.

But my anger soon gives way to a feeling of utter futility. In three weeks I haven't even covered half the distance to the Finnish border and already I have had enough bad experiences and setbacks to bring me to the edge of despair. I feel too tired to keep running, too weary to beg, search, or inquire. Where to turn? To head south would be suicide. I've got to keep going west—but how? I know that beyond Archangel the terrain gets even more desolate, with human settlements few and far apart. I know that escaping from here by boat is my only realistic course. Should I try some more ships? No, they'd all give me the same polite refusal, and I might not be lucky enough to escape the shore patrol a second time.

I leave the harbor and wander through the streets trying to decide my next move. I'm sick with hunger, fatigue, and despair. For the first time since my escape I wish myself back in camp. It would be better to die with Wolff and the others than alone in this godforsaken city where nobody gives a damn.

Across the street I spot a faded, scratched-up signboard leaning against the front wall of an ancient, weatherbeaten house. I can just make out the name "Bormann" on the sign—a German name! I hesitate. Could this be a trap set for escaped German-speaking exiles?

The house is large and must have been stately at one time. I study it carefully before crossing the street. It has a painted tin roof and walls of massive stone blocks. The paint is faded and chipped and the windows are partly covered with paper. It appears to be a private residence.

I walk up to the large, decaying front door and knock cautiously. The name on the sign is Bormann but I decide to play it safe and speak Russian to the person who answers the door.

The door creaks open and a bearded, middle-aged man peers at me inquiringly.

"Good day, sir."

"Good day. Are you calling on me?"

"Yes," I begin uncertainly, "that is, I'm looking for a German."

"Are you German?"

"If you like—" I'm trying to feel him out. "But, Bormann, that's a German name. Are you he?"

He switches to a heavily accented German. "Yes, Bormann. Where are you from and—?"

He gestures for me to enter and indicates a chair. "So, you're German?" He gives me a penetrating look. "You are the first German to come here in years. Until a few years ago there was a small German colony here in the city. Yes, well—the times have scattered them. I'm about the last of them."

My interest is aroused. Forgotten for the moment are my fatigue and the disappointments of the day. I'm speaking to the last remaining German in Archangel!

"And how long have there been—"

"—Germans here?" he anticipates me. "Let's see. Since 1553 or 54 I believe, a whole generation before the city was even founded." He laughs as though he has cracked a good joke. "It was just a trading post then, and the first traders weren't exactly German but English and Dutch. But they were soon followed by German craftsmen who in a relatively short time became well-to-do and respected."

Without being aware of it, Bormann has lapsed into Russian again, which he speaks much more fluently. "My own family lived here for two hundred years. There isn't much left of all that, as you can see." He points to the sparse, shoddy furnishings. On the wall hangs an ancient engraving of what appears to be the famous Crane Tower in Danzig. Beside it is a cheap calendar. In the corner stands an old Black Forest clock and above that a small icon of a saint. He notices my glance and says, a trifle apologetically:

"Yes, my wife is Russian, if its the icon you're looking at. You must know," he hesitates, "that since the Revolution one's nationality doesn't count for much here."

The subject is obviously painful to him. He turns to me. "But you, what wind blows you here?" He is choosing his words carefully.

I tell him, but with a certain amount of circumspection.

Bormann interrupts briskly. "I understand. You aren't the only one in this city who comes from *there* and wants to get *there*," he holds up his hand with thumb and forefinger pointing east and west respectively. Then he averts his eyes. "I'm obliged to tell you, though, that your chances are not good. My advice is that you go back. If you continue west, you're sure to die on the way. Nobody makes it that way." His manner becomes secretive and he switches back to German in a whisper. "Be on your guard. There are all sorts of bounty hunters prowling around here. When bread gets scarce for a guy, he joins the hunt."

I stare at him blankly, not knowing what to say.

His manner grows even more urgent. "Please, follow my advice and go back. There are no transportation facilities here. You can forget the foreign ships. They are too tightly checked and controlled. There are absolutely no trains. And unless you want to risk taking a route through the fishing villages along the coast or the river banks you won't find enough human habitations to enable you to survive. Even the peasants have been forced to become informers—for bread," his hands describe a small square.

Suddenly he remembers something and looks anxiously at the clock. "You'll have to leave, I'm afraid. I'm expecting official visitors . . .." He hesitates again. "Perhaps you could come back later."

The door clicks shut. I'm standing outside again.

Once more I wander through the streets, feeling even more apprehensive after what Bormann has just told me. I have a growing feeling that it's all useless. What chance have I got? Am I waiting for a miracle?

Around three it begins to grow dusk. On impulse I decide to go back to Bormann's. I wonder whether he would be quite so helpless if he knew I had money. If only I did have some money. Let's say half a month's salary from the old days.

Bormann is home. Opposite the door is a mirror. The face I glimpse by the light of the small oil lamp shocks me. I look like a shaggy, filthy ghost of myself.

"Please forgive me for disturbing you again," I begin, "but I just didn't get away today. I wonder if you would allow me to spend the night on the couch over there? It's getting devilish cold out there."

Bormann is sympathetic. "Yes, it is cold." Then in German, "Wait here, we'll see."

A few moments later he returns with another man. "Allow me to introduce a fellow-sufferer. He'll confirm my advice, by the way. This is Mr. Klein. I'll put on the tea, then—" He doesn't finish but disappears into the kitchen.

I shake hands with the stranger. The small, haggard man—probably in his sixties—bows slightly. I am struck by something in his withered face.

"It's cold in Archangel."

"Yes," he agrees, "it's very cold."

The Black Forest clock strikes four.

"There aren't many Germans here."

"Not many."

He's not very communicative.

"May I ask where you come from?"

"Solovki."[2]

From the kitchen comes the metallic rattle of a samovar. Then the sound of coals being poured.

"From Solovki?" I can't believe it.

"Yes, from Solovki."

He walks to the patched window and rises on tiptoe so he can see out into the street. But his eyes seem somewhat remote, as though not focussed on anything specific.

"I was discharged," he adds, as if to himself.

"A long stretch?" I hardly dare ask. I am petrified by the mention of Solovki.

[2]This is the nickname for a group of islands in the White Sea known as the Solovki Islands which have been notorious camps for exiles since the 1920s. For a graphic description of this horrible place see Solzhenitsyn, *Gulag Archipelago II*, pp. 25-70.

"Four years." He paces up and down the room nervously. He doesn't look my way at all.

"And how long since you left?"

He turns and gives me a searching look. "For three months I've been looking for an opportunity . . .." He is arrested by something in my face.

I have it! "Aren't you from the Volga region?"

He halts before me in amazement. "How do you know that?"

I smile. "Judging by your accent, I would guess from the Swabian German settlement there."

"Yes, from Katharinstadt. But—"

"Aha! I knew it." The man before me is thin and withered and much of his face is obscured by his beard, but I remember clearly those expressive eyes.

"Cantor Klein! The Reformation festival in Katharinstadt in 1910. Do you remember?"

Startled, he steps back and studies me carefully. Then his bony face and deep-set eyes light up. He remembers. "Yes, yes," he murmurs, "Pastor Linnemann preached the sermon and the choir sang my own arrangement of the *'Gloria in Excelsis.'* "

"That's right, and a very young high school student turned pages for you at the organ."

"Alexander?"

"It's me."

He continues to stare at me. He can't quite reconcile the scarecrow standing here with his memory of the trimly uniformed youth of long ago. Abruptly, he begins his nervous pacing again, head down, hands working in his pockets. He is agitated. He keeps shaking his head and sighing. He mumbles something under his breath and collapses into a chair.

Like all experienced camp inmates, Cantor Klein has learned to keep the past at a safe distance. A sudden confrontation with it like this is as painful as an unexpected blow in the gut.

During the night Klein and I take turns on the couch. The tea has warmed us up but we are both too nervous to sleep for long at a time. The cantor has regained his composure and in the shared darkness is ready, even eager, to tell about the infamous Solovki.

"The outside world knows nothing about what is going on up there. You can't imagine what human beings are capable of. Before landing there I would not have believed that anyone could treat animals the way people of all races and types are treated in Solovki . . .. Arbitrary beatings are considered trifles—everyone gets used to them. We work ungodly long hours hacking tree stumps out of the frozen ground, for a tiny piece of rotten bread. Or else we receive two salted herrings for the day and are not allowed any water . . ..

In winter, when we collapse from the unbearable cold, we are kicked and clubbed to our feet. Mornings, they drag the sick into the forest even when they are too weak to raise their hands. To those fiendish commissars being sick is shirking—so, special measures. In winter that means being shut up naked in unheated block huts when the temperature stands at minus forty-five to minus fifty-five. In summer they punish us by stripping us naked and tying us to trees where we are beset by swarms of mosquitoes . . . ." He sighs deeply and pauses.

"And the poor women!" He continues. "I never met one who hadn't been sexually abused and maltreated in the most shameful ways by satanic young Chekists. And in the most northerly islands it's supposed to be even more ghastly." He stares into space as though it is all happening before his eyes.

"And the Germans there?"

"I only met one whom I knew to be one. There are no nationalities or ethnic identities there, only a single class of slaves which makes the slavery in all other countries and periods look pale by comparison . . . . All are systematically brutalized and ruined physically and morally when not starved to death outright. God! the suffering that goes on up there—!" He clears his throat. In the darkness it sounds more like a sob.

"And how many are up there?"

"Who can say? There was a pastor—the German I met—who spoke of 50,000, but there may be even more . . . ." From the couch the cantor reaches over to my chair and presses his right hand against my head. "Here, can you feel my thumb is missing? In my despair I hacked it off . . . so as to escape the inhuman labor . . . . Then—they—took me . . ." he breaks off and starts weeping helplessly like a child, in long racking sobs.

Our conversation is over. I sit in the darkness listening to the human sounds of a man in torment and reflect on how much better things are for us on the Mezen by comparison. One should consider it a blessing to have been sent there rather than to Solovki.

Cantor Klein has dropped into an uneasy sleep. It would be cruel to disturb him for my turn on the couch. I try to doze sitting up. The floor is too cold.

Once more I take stock of my situation. I must give it one more try. My only chance, I decide, is to head south. If my luck runs out I can only pray that they'll send me back to Camp 513 rather than the place the cantor has described.

It takes me another three weeks to get to Leningrad, but this stretch is faster and easier than the one to Archangel. By posing as a lumberjack I am able to hitch several long rides on lumber sleigh transports and, farther south, I hop the odd freight train. But the closer I get to the city the scarcer bread seems to get. By the time I finally arrive in Leningrad I am hungrier than I have been in a long time.

Leningrad looks like a city in decay. But, then, which of our cities still looks prosperous? In such cities as Moscow and Kharkov numerous new buildings are cunningly shown to foreign visitors as evidence of business and industrial vitality, when in reality they represent nothing but a sham prosperity. Our cities are as sick as the people—as the regime, which is the source of infection in the first instance!

But Leningrad is a special city; it can be described properly only within the perspective of Russian cultural history. As St. Petersburg it was the elegant creation of Peter the Great. It was a city rising miraculously from northern delta marshes to become the Tsar's "window on Europe", his "Venice of the North." And so it remained down to our times. Then, in a belated gesture inspired by the wartime realization that the city's European influences had embarrassing political implications, its name was Russified to "Petrograd." But the patriotic gesture came too late. Overnight, the Tsar's Russia ceased to exist. Ironically, the Marxist invasion which destroyed it was hatched in the West! So what could be more fitting than that the leading city of the country should now bear the name of a once-obscure Russian who had shaped his revolutionary ideas while in exile in the West.

I walk through the streets of Leningrad shocked and dismayed by what I see. Anyone who knew the city in the old days would scarcely recognize it now. The city's beautiful core between the Fontanka Canal and Neva River, with its eighteenth-century glories, looks dilapidated and neglected. There are cheap attempts to hide the disintegration behind serried rows of Red street flags and huge propaganda posters and banners. But these vulgar displays serve only to emphasize the city's lost splendor.

The people in the streets look not only impoverished and dispirited, but *furtive* somehow, as though they are aware of being watched and hunted. If free people look so oppressed what must I, an escaped exile, look like? I consider my position nervously as I wander down the famous Nevsky Prospect. What has happened to its colorful life with the gaily dressed, hurrying crowds, the fancy carriages and cars, and the splendid shops? I glance up relieved to see that the glass globe atop the dome of the Singer Sewing Machine building is still there although it is no longer revolving. The huge sphere was a somewhat vulgar but affectionately tolerated symbol of Leningrad's pre-war prosperity.

I pass the renowned Café Nord, where the cream of Russian and European aristocracy once dined in state. The restaurant is still open but appears to have fallen on bad times. The exotic displays of pastry which once graced its windows have dwindled to a few artificial-looking cakes. Nevertheless the thought of food makes me gaze longingly at the doors. What I wouldn't give for just a few crumbs from the tables inside. The dull ache in my gut leaps to flame. I must get a piece of bread somewhere!

Suddenly I am overtaken by a noisy shoal of *bezprizorniki*. They swarm around me like hungry young sharks. But they are not after me; their practised beggars' eyes have already dismissed me. They are after real game: a well-dressed man in European clothes walking just ahead of me. I have been following him myself, hoping for a chance to address him and perhaps ask him for a few kopeks for bread. Two of the ragamuffins, both wearing rakish Tatar caps and long tattered coats, accost the European by dancing around him and accompanying their chattering appeals with graphic gestures. The man shakes his head and keeps on walking, apparently unconcerned. He seems to be used to this kind of assault.

But the two waifs persist. I am close enough to hear their bad Russian. One of them starts shouting at the European in broken German:

"You . . . got . . . brad? Piece brad, sir—give me—" he spreads his fingers. The smaller child takes up the chant in Russian.

"Bread? Money? Bread?"

The bigger lad must be German.

The besieged man stops on the corner to cross the street. I catch a glimpse of his white shirt, well-cut overcoat, and polished shoes. He has a smooth, pink face and a self-assured air. He must be a Westener here on a business trip. He tries to shoo the boys away in German. "Nothing! I have nothing for you. Go—or I call the police."

The boys understand the reference to police and stop their antics. The man crosses the street but the boys make no attempt to follow. For a moment I'm tempted to try my luck with him. But a glance at the rags I'm wearing is enough to deter me. No! He'll take me for a professional beggar too and give me the same treatment. I watch as the man continues down the street on the other side, then turns into a building. Another image of the free West has come and gone tantalizingly before my eyes.

From a safe distance, the two street urchins are hurling juicy Russian obscenities after the European. They are standing on the corner waving their fists and cursing. The rest of their comrades are already far down the street.

I turn to the older lad and address him in German. "Where do you come from?"

He gives me a crafty wink. "Uh—from Siberia." He utters another Russian curse.

"Are you German?"

He laughs airily. "Ja—me Gairman! Mine family—they be kill—in Siberia."

It's an odd mixture of German, Tatar, and Russian.

"What's your name then?"

He rummages around in his enormous coat pocket and shows me a dirty scrap of paper. "Krieger, Pyotr," he points to the name on the paper. Written in Russian, the name is, in fact, Krueger. The address is a village in the Siberian province of Tomsk.

The boy looks at me expectantly, as though something should come of this identification. Suddenly he tears the paper out of my hand and runs off, followed by the other boy. The ragged soles of their boots smack along the icy street. Then I too see the policeman come strolling along.

I cross the street casually and start walking in the opposite direction.

I'm already discovering just how tough things are in the big city for fugitives like me. The shortage of food is bad enough, but the danger of arrest is even worse. The streets are swarming not only with policemen in uniform but with GPU men as well who are very conspicuous even if they are dressed in plain clothes. These sharp-eyed predators are extremely adept, I've been told, at spotting escapees and other likely victims among the populace.

I keep walking and thinking how very tired I am of being on the run. And I am desperate for something to eat. I wander into the less frequented side streets. Towards evening I fall in with three other men who are clearly fugitives of one kind or another. They are tight-lipped about themselves, but invite me to join them for the night. I accompany them to a narrow, dark alley in a sleazy quarter of the city. We stop at a crude shelter in a dirty, littered corner. The shelter is nothing more than a makeshift lean-to put up with a few old boards and other odds and ends either scrounged or stolen.

The men share a bit of moldy bread with me and give me half of a not-very-fresh- herring. From their rough joking I gather that one of them has had a bit of light-fingered luck somewhere. We huddle together under a few frayed old gunny sacks, newspapers, and a tattered horse blanket. It's cold but bearable.

In the morning I thank my companions of the night and strike off on my own again. I do not want to survive by becoming a derelict.

I know I am near the end of the line. A deep, sullen apathy settles down over me. I just don't care anymore.

I drag myself along the streets and finally down to the harbor. As I stand and gaze yearningly at the ships someone taps me on the shoulder. I know without turning around that this is it. The two harbor guards ask me a few perfunctory questions and decide to turn me over to the GPU.

I feel nothing but profound relief that it is finally over.

The GPU building to which I am taken is as dazzling as a theatre with its garishly lighted interior. We pass through many wide corridors with high ceilings. People are coming and going and everybody seems to be in a hurry. The atmosphere is that of a busy commercial office.

I am conducted into a large, spartanly furnished room where two officials are seated at their desks in front of high, fancily ornamented windows. This building must have been some aristocrat's mansion in former times. The younger man is slim and dark, amiable and refined of manner, obviously an educated Russian. The older one is a bulky, awkward man with shaggy eyebrows and a bulbous nose. There is something odd about him. When he speaks I know what it is: his execrable Russian betrays him as a foreigner.

The young Russian opens the interrogation with friendly, routine questions: What circumstances have brought me to Leningrad? Where did I come from and what did I intend to do here? These polite queries are interspersed with cruder, more direct questions from the older man. It becomes a kind of cross examination. I have made up my mind to admit only that I am an escaped convict and to reveal as little as possible about my past before being exiled.

"So you are—? the Russian inquires politely

"An escaped exile."

"That is," he coughs delicately, "a voluntary resettler, according to your own declaration."

"A voluntary resettler, yes," I correct myself.

"A German?"

"Yes, a German."

"Aha—so you are a *kulak* then," the foreigner interrupts in good German. "And you've decided to exchange your state service in the North for the roving life, what?" The heavy eyebrows gather in a scowl. "That will hardly shorten your stay in Archangel." He has switched back to Russian again.

The Russian smiles, but not at the joke.

"And exactly what were you going to do here?" the European pursues.

I despise this Westerner who has come here to work for the Soviets, but I must watch myself. "I wanted to get out—away from there—anywhere else, but away. Do you know what it's like up there?"

The European looks hard at me, his eyes showing surprise. My candid answers apparently do not fit standard procedure here. He decides to meet candor with candor.

"Yeah, I understand all right. You are one of those fools who dreams of life in the West. Do you think that I, and thousands more like me, would leave the West to come here if it was such a paradise there?" The eyebrows bristle in lofty contempt. "What do you know about conditions in Germany, or anywhere else, you miserable son-of-a-bitch?" He utters a short mocking laugh.

I choke back an angry retort. I remember Klein! Solovki! I let my head sink in silence. I am weary to my soul.

"Do you want to go back to the Mezen?" the Russian is as polite as ever.

"Yes, please—back."

The freight train is again rolling north. The familiar, hateful "clack-clack—clack" is deadening my tired brain. In our car there are about thirty Russians, including some wives and children. It's all depressingly similar to a year and a half ago, except that these people are even more weary and starved-looking than we were. Brooding and silent, they seem to accept their fate without complaint. From time to time somebody sighs or crosses himself.

Most of these people come from Kharkov, where they lived close to the city in small villages. They were "determined" for the North because of their refusal to allow themselves to be collectivized. They tell their sad story matter-of-factly; their calm fatalism excludes any attempt at self-justification.

Interest is now centered on the camps. They want me to tell them what it's like. Already they are reconciled to bearing their lot up there. They are stoic but not indifferent. What a capacity for suffering the Slavs have compared with us Germans. With their submissive faces and melancholy eyes they accept pain, hardship, and oppression as their natural lot. They are both easy-going and stubborn, but they seldom yield to despair. They endure their hard lives with good will and die uncomplainingly.

Beside me sits a Russian village teacher wearing a mangy suit of what was once English tweed. He is well-read and has a thorough knowledge of the great Russian writers, including the forbidden ones now banned. The young man and I discuss literature and debate ideas for hours on end. By the time we pass through Vologda our friendship has progressed to the point where he proudly exhibits his home-made balalaika. Over the rattle of the train he sings the haunting songs of his people. He plays and sings beautifully and all of us listen gratefully. The peasants from Kharkov start joining in on the choruses and soon we have a regular choir providing expert accompaniment to the soloist.

After the young teacher has finally put away his balalaika I reflect on the special magic of Russian folk songs. What makes them so haunting, so achingly beautiful? They seem to grow right out of the Russian soil, as natural as the steppe grass, as hardy as the wild pear trees. And yet they are suffused with strange, mystical moods and a serene fatalism that defies analysis. In my mind, I try translating one of the teacher's songs, a traditional song about the Volga.

> In Russia's wide expanses
> Who can find a corner,
> Where the peasant is not sorrow-worn
> Where the sower does not reap affliction?
>> Who is singing by the Volga?
>> Barge men pulling on the bank
>> Try to ease their misery in song,
>> Their music interspersed with groans.
> Volga—Volga—when spring comes
> Your waters flow in torrents
> Over earth and sand.
> But mightier yet are streams
> Of tears from people,
> Flooding all the land.

I work a long time at my translation, but I know I have not managed to capture the unique quality of the original. A translation could never capture that unique flavor. German is not the natural vehicle of Russian experience, of Russian melancholy. And yet we German-Mennonites have stolidly and perversely tried for generations to live our Russian experience in a foreign language.

Vologda—Vjatka—Kotlas. The names have a sinister ring. Many thousands pass through these places going north. But few, if any, ever pass through them going south.

This second journey is just as monotonous and even more painful for me than the first one was. Inside, the endless swaying; outside, the eternal forest stands immobile and unchanged. I have seen and experienced it all before and can tell the others what to expect. And that's what makes it more painful: I know what to expect. From my soul I pity these innocent victims who gaze, almost longingly, at the endless rows of trees gliding by. I know only too well what these trees conceal.

Sometime around the end of April—I have lost interest in time and dates—we reach Camp Number 513 for voluntary resettlers.

I am home again.

Part Four
More Than Bread

Our transport leader takes me straight to Comma.

"Ah, my little rabbit, here you are!" he greets me jovially. "You took a big jump. Look, the calendar says May third. You've been hopping around out of your cage for four months. Ha-ha-ha. And now we've got you by the hind legs again."

He stops laughing and leans forward. "But you are a very lucky little rabbit, as it turns out. We have been notified to take back all first-time escapees without special punishment." He gives me a long, hard look. "But if you try it again, you'll be a very dead rabbit." He is not smiling now. "You can go back to your old barrack."

I feel relief, but little more. Remarkably decent of them. But perhaps there's some nasty trick behind it all. I'll have to be on my guard.

Barrack Number 7 appears empty. Everyone is working. Only Ohm Peters is in his bunk, wrapped in his fur coat, coughing—exactly as I left him four months ago. When he sees me come in his rheumy old eyes widen in surprise. He lifts a weak hand in greeting.

"You're back Alexander?" His wasted face is as warm and friendly as ever.

I look down at the dear old man and I want to weep. "Yes, Ohm Jasch, but I don't know for how much longer." I try not to sound bitter.

"Where have you been then?" He gives my hand a weak squeeze.

"In Archangel and Leningrad mostly. I'm very tired and discouraged, Ohm Jasch."

"Tired, discouraged—yes . . ." he echoes in a whisper. "But at least you're still alive." He digs a piece of bread out of the straw sack that serves him as a pillow.

"Here take it, you must be hungry."

He is overtaken by another fit of coughing and doesn't hear my murmured refusal. He continues to hold out the bread and I am forced to accept it.

The old man tries to sit up. I help him. "A lot of things have happened here Sasha. Two weeks ago we buried poor Maria Koehn—typhus. Only a day or two later Mrs. Preuss died in the hospital. And, it hurts me to tell you, our dear Martha is also gone—at the end of January. Volodya Wolff has taken it very hard. But they had their wedding—when it was obvious she would not—they both insisted. I felt it to be my duty, Sasha, even though we all knew it could not be for long. But I worry about Volodya. He is not his old self."

So Martha and Maria are gone. How awful for Wolff and Koehn. I feel guilty about not having been here to share their grief. How like Wolff to insist on a symbolic marriage to his dying bride.

I sit down and look around the barrack. "So our ranks are thinner," I think out loud.

"Were," Peters amends. "We have two more Russians and a Tatar with us now. But I'm sure you'll be able to get your old bunk back again."

Right now I don't care about my old bunk; I am wrestling with my own despair. I can tell from the few things the old man has told me that the situation here has deteriorated in my absence, that our prospects are even bleaker. How can I possibly face this wretched existence again?

"Ohm Jasch, I feel as if I'm getting close to the end of my rope too."

It's as though he has expected me to say that. The old man's power of discernment and strength of spirit are as remarkable as ever. He leans forward his eyes full of love and gentle concern.

"God is a mysterious God, Alexander. By nature we are all fainthearted grumblers." His eyes are full of conviction. "Do you know when all that will cease?" His hand describes a feeble arc, then drops. "When we finally grasp the truth that the Righteous One is waiting for us at the end of the road. Now it's true our road is very hard, but He expects us to look beyond our own miseries to Him. God can't smooth that road for us, Sasha. He can only wait for us at the end of it . . . ."

I lean back on the bunk and listen to the old man as though from a great distance. His words fall on my parched spirit like a gentle rain. My mood of hopelessness begins to lift a little. Perhaps I owe it to myself, and to the others, to continue the struggle a little longer and look beyond my own miseries, as the old man says in his trusting way.

When Wolff comes in I am shocked at how much he has aged during the months I've been gone. His dark curly hair and beard are threaded with white; his face and eyes are pale and lustreless.

"So the prodigal son has returned," he tries to joke after getting over the surprise of seeing me again. "I'm afraid we have no fatted calf to offer you though, Sasha." He embraces me and shakes my hand warmly.

I draw him aside to commiserate with him over Martha.

"Yes, my friend," he says simply. "She was my last anchor, and she's gone. I'm drifting now, Sasha, drifting. I don't know how long . . . ." His voice breaks and he turns away.

Koehn, Tielmann, and the others come over to greet me. I shake Koehn's hand silently. He understands.

"Maria's struggles are over, Sasha. If it weren't for the kids, I'd like nothing better than to join her." He swallows hard and his eyes fill with tears.

Tielmann also looks older and more debilitated. I can see that he is on borrowed time, although he tries valiantly to be cheerful and hearty in my presence.

The friendly greetings do not deceive me. The faces around me tell the true story. These four months have taken a toll on these people that frightens me. The air of defeat in the barrack is almost palpable. I sense that these people have abandoned hope, that they are simply going through the motions of living as they await their inevitable end.

Wolff understands my mood. "You musn't mind us, Sasha. We're all a little stir-crazy. After all, we haven't had the benefit of a relaxing winter holiday like some people." He slaps my shoulder, but without the old force. "Now tell us all about your excursion, my friend."

Just before my return, they tell me, there had been a big May Day celebration. The camp inmates were given the signal honor of working on the holiday without receiving their usual bread rations, which were to be "donated" to the state. As compensation, Comma magnanimously declared that May fifteenth would be a rest day.

When the day comes we do not even bother to get away from camp by going for a long walk as we had done on previous rest days. The malignant mood of resignation among us has spread too far. We prefer to remain in our bunks and brood.

Ohm Peters tries to get us out of our apathy by holding a service. Remarkably, everyone attends. Even the two Russians and Father Nikolai are there.

It is dark and gloomy in the barrack. The low heat of the stove is not really warming. The assembled people sit beside each other on the bunks, heads down, hands lying limply in their laps. Even the usual shuffling of feet and clearing of throats are strangely absent. We sit numbly in our rags as Ohm Peters' scratchy voice slowly but reverently brings alive the one hundred and thirty-ninth Psalm.

"—'if I make my bed in hell, behold thou art there.' "

Suddenly Neufeld is on his feet, his leathery face contorted, black eyes blazing a crazed look.

"God! God! That's all I ever hear from you pious bastards. What God? Where is he in this freezing hell? Call yourselves Christians—you smug hypocrites? When we still had our one thousand acres we were all fine Christians—at least on Sundays. That bullshit is over now—for good!" His voice rises to a demented scream. "*Bread*, that's our Jesus here!"

He reaches out and grabs Peters' Bible. "You can't eat this, you old fool, so what good is it?" He holds the book up in front of Ohm Jasch's calm face; then in a surprising display of strength he tears the book in half, the pages flying, and hurls the pieces to the floor.

"It's all a fraud, you gullible fools. We're all freezing and starving here, and you listen to this old *Fromma* reading words to you—aaaahn! Well, I've had enough. I'm going." He glares around balefully, then heads for the door. "Shit on you—!" he shouts harshly over his shoulder and stamps out.

We sit there stunned, looking at each other. Ohm Peters is already on his knees gathering the scattered parts of his precious Bible. We help him, and when he has the broken book safely in his hands again he sits down and turns back to us, as calm and collected as before. Mrs. Neufeld sits stony-faced in the corner. She has not moved. Ohm Jasch gives her a look of deep compassion.

"We must not condemn our brother Neufeld for his outburst. He needs our compassion, not our condemnation. His despair is also a cry for help, and we must listen to that cry.

"None of us has the strength to stave off despair without God's help. Let us remember that. He is there, in spite of everything. In our situation here we have all been led to the far edge of suffering and desperation—to the point where we either give up in despair or give in to Him! Here we are forced to become either praisers or scoffers, my friends."

Ohm Peters has finished as quietly and confidently as he began. We close by praying an old church hymn:

Oh let thy word remain
With us Redeemer dear:
In grace to be our gain,
Both yonder and down here.

I glance at the tattered figures around me, bony hands folded, tired eyes shut in their emaciated faces. I see now that I was wrong about these people: they may look defeated, but they have not yet given up completely. For all their suffering there is still a spark of hope, a yearning for something more than bread. Perhaps there will be others among us who will fall from despair into blasphemy like Neufeld, but there is an inner strength in evidence here, a spiritual reserve that is far from exhausted. There is a faith at work in these people which is capable of surviving much more than Neufeld's desperate contempt and bitter ridicule.

Next morning Neufeld's bed is empty. He has been away all night and his wife is worried. She prevails upon several of us to go looking for him in the little time we have before going to work. We spread out through our compound but find no sign of him.

Nor does he show up at the work site. At noon we are greeted with the ugly news that Neufeld's body has been found in the forest. He had hanged himself with the piece of rope he used as a belt. He was found with his ragged old pants dangling around his feet.

Neufeld has paid the price. I recall Wolff's angry denunciation of him as a Judas. But Wolff makes no mention of his remark and I do not remind him.

Comma has brought in a brigade of *udarniki* as shock workers to "intensify" our work. These "beaters" are the terror of Russian factory workers. We have heard about them but none of us has ever seen them. The summoning of the *udarniki*, we are told, is designed as a reprimand and a warning to us. Apparently, our production in the last six months has fallen well below expectations. These people are to show us how much our production can be increased.

Next morning we find the advertised brigade of shock workers—twenty vigorous, well-nourished, and warmly clad young men—assembled at our work site. The sight of them causes us to stop and stare. Koehn, Wolff, and I look at each other: how long has it been since we saw so many physically normal-looking people at one time?

Their movements are full of energy and purpose. They go to work eagerly. Koehn and I are still on our first log when the two nearest us are already cutting their third tree.

"Don't rise to the challenge," Wolff calls across to us in German. "Considering the crumbs we get, we're doing three times as much. In any case, here's another example of how you can bury your conscience—given enough bread." He nods his head in the direction of the *udarniki.*

"What d'ya mean bury your conscience with bread?" One of them speaks fluent German. He's clearly annoyed and sets down his axe. "Explain yourself, you turd."

Wolff hesitates a perceptible moment. "It's like this, friend. First you guys allow yourselves to be well fed and beefed up, and then you're paraded before your famished countrymen as model workers. If you had to live on our watery soup and bit of bread your enthusiasm wouldn't last long."

The young worker's face runs through an almost comical set of expressions. At first he looks shocked, then bewildered, and finally angry. He is torn between a better understanding of our situation and contempt for us as exiles. He glares at Wolff a long moment. "Damn *kulaks,*" he finally mutters and turns back to work.

I signal Wolff to shut up. He's said too much already.

"The main thing," Tielmann says firmly, "is not to let them bluff us now. None of us cuts one more log than before—otherwise they've got us."

It starts to rain. The rags we have wrapped around our torn shoes don't keep out the water. It seeps through the rents with every step. Tielmann pulls off his soaked woollen jacket and wrings it out. His shirt is tattered beyond belief. His pants are held up by a few strings of twine twisted together—too flimsy for Neufeld's purpose, I can't help thinking. Tielmann folds and refolds his jacket in order to wring more water out of it.

"Even a European jacket can't absorb all the rain that pours from a Russian sky," Wolff comments.

Our noon break has to be used mainly to dry our wet clothes on the stove. We handle the thin remnants of our clothing carefully, lest they disintegrate in our hands. The shabby shirts, looking for all the world like the clothes one might put on scarecrows, are hung up in the room to dry.

In the afternoon the weather gets colder. The rain is transformed into moist, fluffy snow. We are glad we have managed to dry our clothes at least partially.

"If you can't get warm by working, I'll lead you in a brisk set of calisthenics," Wolff sneers as we shiver.

A week later the *udarniki* disappear as suddenly as they came. They have been moved to another camp to radiate vitality and dedication among starving exiles.

Tielmann is losing his teeth, one after the other. He has only about half a dozen left. The lack of nourishing food, especially fats, wears down even the strongest of us. Comma gives Tielmann permission to go to Andreievka, but they don't have dental facilities there and refer the sick man to Vologda.

"Actually, false teeth are just a luxury here," Tielmann says wryly. "What does a man need false teeth for when there's nothing to chew anyway." But he goes.

A week later he is back. He is in possession of new teeth, but he is so weak from his dental ordeal that he has to be taken off the work list. He utilizes his meagre strength to gather firewood for the barrack. He is able to do that for another week; then he is forced to remain in his bunk.

"How are things, Diedka?" I greet him one evening.

"Coming to an end, Sasha—but it's all right." His voice is weak, but he is calm and self-possessed. "You know, it's funny," he continues, "the deeper we sink here the more personal and vivid one's past becomes."

He turns away, trying to control himself. His hands are badly swollen; even his face looks bloated. I want to persuade him to go to the hospital, but I sense that it is too late. He speaks in the heavy, slurred tones of one who is seriously ill. Nevertheless, he wants to talk.

"Do you remember when I gave up my school, Sasha?" At the time you all regarded it as a heroic act. But I don't mind telling you now that it wasn't quite such a simple moral problem for me as it seemed. Privately, I went through a rough battle. Seven, eight years of exposure to Bolshevik ideology while closed off from a healthier outside world had had their effect on me. The despairing farmers all around me, plus the numerous disappointments we idealists had suffered—all that made me waver. There were moments when I was ready to give in, to give the new Soviet school a try. I told myself I could keep mum and make the necessary compromises. To take that course would have been so much easier. But then . . . the ugly realities of our society again flooded in on my consciousness. I sat at my desk and reminded myself that once I had surrendered my Mennonite principles there would be no going back for me. I would have to go all the way . . . . Sasha, I just couldn't have done that—no, for better or worse, I had to make my stand.

"But I didn't feel like a hero after I had resigned, I can tell you. I regretted my decision for a long time. Being deprived of my classroom was the worst thing that ever happened to me. Nothing that has happened to me since—even this—has shaken me so badly, made me so unsure of myself. Looking back I can see that my real life ended at that point—the rest has been just a bad dream that doesn't really matter very much."

He tries to prop himself up on his elbow, but he can't. He has exhausted himself, and there is nothing I can do for him except listen to him.

"Sasha, I must tell you one more thing." He begins to sob weakly. "I—I—I'm sorry now that I didn't co-operate with the authorities . . .. What did I gain by rebelling? What did I accomplish? Nothing! It all came to nothing."

His face is flushed with emotion and the effort of speaking. He lies back with a long sigh, his energy utterly spent.

"You did what you had to, Diedka," I murmur consolingly. "You did what you regarded as right—and you'd do it the same way again."

I take his hand and sit with him until he has fallen asleep.

An old Russian peasant with a long, scraggy beard stands in front of our barrack door during the dinner hour one day. He is a walking corpse. His fur coat is even scraggier than his beard and his pants flutter in tatters around his calves. His feet are wrapped in filthy rags held together with bast thongs. His eyes are sunken black pools and his emaciated body keeps trembling and twitching as he stands leaning on his stick. The shrill wisp of a voice that emerges from this apparition is barely human:

"For Christ's sake, a piece . . . bread."

Wolff breaks in half the bread ration he has just received and gives it to him. "You're in luck grandfather. You've hit the affluent part of camp, comparatively speaking. Our clothes have only a few fashionable tears—to show we're honest working class people. Even our boots proclaim our superior status." He points down: the soles of his boots are tied to the uppers with strings and rags and are lined with braided bast for warmth.

The beggar sways on his stick and stares at Wolff, not comprehending the joke. He crosses himself shakily and wobbles off, chewing greedily on his bread.

"Well, Volodya," I mutter, "it's still possible to surpass our condition, I see."

"Yeah, but only on the far side of the superlative degree."

On the way back to work he is thoughtful. "Did you notice that the old scarecrow still crossed himself? You could argue it's just habit, of course, but it isn't. Even a pitiful human wreck like that takes comfort in being in touch with something bigger than himself. How can the Communists stamp out that kind of instinct, the deep human urge not only to satisfy all-consuming hunger but to do it with God's blessing . . . to . . . to eat at the Lord's table, so to speak?"

"But Volodya, the Soviets will in time erase all memory of the Lord's table. How many more Father Nikolais will Soviet society produce? He belongs to a dying breed—like the rest of us. Priests are as obsolete in our new society as the old landowners—or Mennonite colonists. And when all the Father Nikolais are gone, the churches will also be gone and with them the congregations of believers. And then starving beggars will no longer make the sign of the cross."

"And people like you and me will be an extinct species too—and so we won't care either," Wolff adds with a grim laugh. "Well, Philosopher, you may be right, but somehow I don't think it'll be that simple. They may control the peasant by brute force, but they'll never change his basic nature—he's too stubborn. And, Sasha, he's a born believer—always has been, always will be. And it's the same with us Mennonites. They can starve us and kill us in places like this, but they'll never make atheists out of us."

I remain silent. Has Wolff forgotten about Neufeld?

The coming of mid-summer is once again accompanied by hordes of insects. It's impossible to get rid of the swarms of mosquitoes. We gather masses of willow leaves, dry them on the oven, and roll them into thick cigarettes with newsprint. The smoke proves to be the best protection against these pesky insects.

The nights, however, are excruciating torture-sessions. Mosquitoes, earth fleas, and especially lice, plague us and we can never quite rid ourselves of these pests, even in winter. During the nights, when I am awakened by the insect invasion, I hear scratching and grumbling on all sides. In the morning the children have bloody spots all over their bodies. We try to maintain a smudge in the oven at night by putting green leaves and small pine branches on the coals, but the smoke doesn't draw properly and makes it almost impossible to breathe in the already fetid barrack.

Once again I write to my relatives in Germany, but my distaste for writing begging letters has grown to the point where I can bring myself to ask only for remedies against the insects.

Tielmann is dying. One of our convalescents comes to the work site to tell me. I run as fast as my weakened limbs allow, but I am soon so overcome with vertigo and nausea that I have to sit down and rest to ease my churning stomach and pounding heart. I drag myself the rest of the way, terrified that I may collapse before I get there.

"There you are Sasha." He recognizes me but his voice sounds like an exhalation.

Still panting and dizzy, I sit down beside him and feel his forehead. It is as dry and hot as a flatiron. I stroke his hand gently, but he winces. My calloused hand must feel like sandpaper to him.

I want to say something loving to him, do something for him. But I can't think of anything, so I offer him the rest of my bread. It's an absurd gesture, I know, but his faint smile shows that he understands.

"Don't need bread anymore . . . that kind," he gasps. "Sasha, write. Tell them . . . I was . . . reconciled." His voice fails him.

I look around wildly. Ohm Peters, whose help has always been available, now, in an emergency when someone is dying, appears to be sleeping. A mosquito buzzes against the window. From the forest the sound of axe strokes is faint and muffled. My head is reeling. I try to focus on Tielmann's face, but my eyes don't seem to be functioning properly.

I fumble for his trembling hand, close my eyes, and start reciting the Lord's Prayer aloud. But the words get fuzzy and then vanish as a terrible wave of nausea engulfs me. I feel myself falling, falling towards the pale oval below me on the bed.

When I wake up it is a week later. Apparently I had been delirious with fever for most of that time, but now I have passed the crisis. Everything seems at a great remove from me. Mrs. Zimmerman brings me a mug of hot tea and holds it for me as my lips tremble towards solid touch again. The tea is so good I begin to slobber greedily, oblivious to the searing heat on my tongue. But the reek of the Zimmerman woman's body close to my face is almost more than I can bear. I thank her weakly and sink back on my straw sack.

Somebody is loudly announcing the arrival of packages. Wolff hands me my notice with his old half-grin. I read it over and over. I even count the number of words—nine words printed on poor paper: my name and the Camp address. Then I remember.

Painfully, I twist my head and shoulders to the right. Tielmann's bunk is empty. I forget my parcel as I mourn for my old friend and remember the circumstances of our last moments together.

In the afternoon Wolff and Koehn and some others go to fetch the parcels. That evening, for the first time in months, one again hears happy exclamations from lucky recipients. From my bunk I see a child's hand plunge into a gift box and greedily stuff something into its mouth.

"Peter!" Mrs. Zimmermann admonishes anxiously, "you're spilling the beautiful rice." She stops to gather the precious spilled grains. The little one, munching with ecstatic concentration, doesn't even hear her.

"Can't you wait? We'll cook some right away."

"Right away," the children echo and follow their mother's every move like ferrets.

Wolff places my package before me on the bed with a triumphant flourish. "A bit of luck," he chuckles. "The thief at the post office wanted the honor of a personal visit from you, but we finally persuaded him you were unable to appear just now. So—no duty!"

The rustle of broken strings and paper. Then the heavenly aroma of groceries. I prop myself up and breath in the smells slowly and voluptuously.

Wolff is delighted. "Even a patient can't satisfy his hunger through his nose. Sasha, listen: a kilogram of rice." He opens the bag. I let the grains trickle through my fingers like a pasha playing with his gems. I put a grain between my teeth and crunch it with a delicious snap.

"There's flour here too." Wolff puffs flour dust into my face. He's a good nurse.

"A piece of bacon!" he exults. "Now you can let out your belt again. That's the stuff that pot bellies are made of, old campaigner."

For a whole week, noon and evening, I am able to supplement the kitchen soup with rations from my package. Often I imagine I can feel new strength. At such times I sit up and gaze at the magnificent trees in the forest through the hole that serves as my window. But when I recall the oppressive, agonizing hours I have spent cutting timber, I am so overcome with frustration and despair that I fall back on my pillow convinced that further struggle is futile.

The gang is back from work.

"Have you heard they intend to release children under twelve, old people over sixty, and invalids?" Koehn says.

"Yeah," Wolff scoffs, "I've heard something like that. But don't get your hopes up for nothing. Except for Ohm Jasch, we're all under sixty, and as for invalids—well, we're still classified as robust specimens, paragons of health and vigor."

"What do you mean healthy?"

"Simple. On the camp list everybody who can still walk or stand up is classified as healthy. If you chop off your leg you're an invalid, but then they'll take off your head too." Wolff makes the appropriate gesture. "Naw, old pal. They're not going to ease us into retirement yet. Anyway," his voice drops, "where could we go? Back to the Volga as stateless persons? Forget it!"

Wolff whistles through his teeth. It is a sign that he is perturbed.

Anna Zimmermann has appointed herself my special nurse during my convalescence. In the evening, when she is not busy with her children, she hovers about my bed trying to anticipate needs I have not yet thought of and chatters away about things in which I have no interest. She means well, probably, but I find her hearty solicitude oppressive. I sense something a little forced if not designing in her manner. I would much prefer having Wolff around me. From his bunk Wolff regards me with sardonic amusement as Mrs. Zimmermann swoops and darts to serve me. I know he is aware of my embarrassment, but he makes no attempt to rescue me from the woman's unwanted attendance.

Sad to say, the brutal months of camp life have taken their toll on Mrs. Zimmermann. She has coarsened physically as the result of the hard work in the forest, and she has lost the soft charm and femininity she had when she came. Her auburn hair is untidy and she exudes the same sour body odor as the rest of us do. She is as devoted as ever to her three children, but the constant struggle to provide them and herself with sufficient nourishment has hardened her and made her shrill and aggressive. She is domineering towards the other women, wheedling with the men. As much as I sympathize with her plight, I feel vaguely uneasy in her presence.

Today, as usual, she has taken her children to the nursery and gone to work with the others. Around mid-morning I am dozing in my bunk when the door opens and Anna Zimmermann comes in. She walks slowly to her bunk sighing heavily. She lies down and a few moments later I hear her muffled sobbing. She must be sick. I feel sorry for her. I should at least show my concern and ask her what is wrong. But somehow I can't bring myself to address her. I keep my eyes closed and doze off again.

When I open my eyes I see Mrs. Zimmermann's tear-stained face above me. How long has she been standing there?

"How are things going, Alexander Andreievitch?" She is speaking Russian.

I try to keep it light. "Well, they're still going. I suppose they could be even worse."

She sits down on Tielmann's empty bunk. She looks agitated. Her face is flushed and she is twisting something nervously in her hands. I feel uncomfortable. What's wrong with the woman?

"How long can we go on like this?" she blurts out suddenly. "My God, it's all so . . . ." She turns away from me and tries to choke back her tears.

Poor woman. Her anguish breaks down my reserve. "Yes, Anna Ivanovna, I know how you feel. It must be even harder for you, with the children and . . . ."

Sobbing piteously, she throws herself down beside my bunk. She squeezes my hand and gives me a beseeching look. "Alexander, please help me. I'll pay you back, I promise—anyway you like." She buries her face against my shoulder, racked by violent sobs.

My first impulse is to tell the poor, desperate creature to get away from me. But my anger and revulsion are too strongly mixed with compassion—and shame. Camp life is bad enough for a man, but that it should do this to a once proud, refined woman and mother is too horrible. The shame I feel is for myself as a man. That my Liese might have been forced to fight for survival in this way in similar circumstances is a thought I cannot bear. No, I can't add to the woman's suffering by saying something cruel to her.

Yet the whole scene including her nursing services, has been so deliberately staged. If her anguish is real, so is her scheming. She has chosen to approach me at just this time because she knew there would be no one else in the barrack. Ohm Peters always goes for a walk around mid-morning and there is no one else about. But I have no right to be harsh in my judgement. I think of her children.

Gently, I lift her head from my shoulder, release my hand from hers, reach under my bunk, and give her the rest of my bag of flour.

"Here, take it—for the children. There is nothing to pay back. Now, please, I'm very tired."

She accepts the flour with extravagant expressions of gratitude. I just want her to go and leave me alone.

I decide not to tell Wolff about the incident.

My physical strength is slowly coming back, but I dread the thought of returning to work in the forest. This isolated wilderness with its dozen barracks scattered about, their tattered, emaciated inmates forced to wield axes and saws for long hours, their late home-coming to a meal of watery soup and adulterated bread—just thinking of this ugly scene plunges me into deep gloom. Not that lying on my bunk here is much better! I'm spared the physical abuses, but my mind and memory are too active and threaten to get out of hand at times. During the day I am usually plunged into memories of the past which make the miserable present seem even worse. During the night I have nightmares about the present and the future. Our birch grove cemetery is becoming the central symbol of our experience here. No matter how hard we struggle, the birches will have us in the end and will some day be nodding over our sightless eyes.

Only when the others return from work in the evening—Wolff with his refreshing witticisms, Koehn with his warmth and good sense, Father Nikolai with his unflagging spirituality—only at these times do my black thoughts subside for an hour or two to allow me to see that life in the present is still possible, bitter hard though it is. These evening hours are the cherished part of our day.

Our conversations during this time are not always about food parcels and working conditions. More and more we find ourselves discussing political and philosophical topics. Even the two Russians, who for a long time conversed almost exclusively with Father Nikolai, now come over and chat with the rest of us. As a result, our discussions are almost always in Russian. German seems less appropriate to our circumstances.

One of the two Russians is a lean, leathery old cavalry officer who is inordinately fond of Dostoevsky and likes to apply the great master's moral insights to every conceivable subject and situation. Anatoly Mironovitch is convinced that the prophecies in Dostoevsky's novels await inevitable fulfillment.

As we have so often done before, we are once again discussing Russia's future in the light of her contemporary situation. And as usual, the old officer is invoking the voice of his revered master: "How does Feodor Mikhailovitch" (he always refers to Dostoevsky by first name and patronymic, as though he had known him personally) "put it? 'That strange things will happen in Russia, that everywhere people will be talking about God?' "

"Yes, and in atheistic Russia too," the priest adds with quiet conviction.

Wolff also knows his Dostoevsky. He quotes from *The Brothers Karamazov:* " '. . . an unbelieving reformer will never do anything in Russia, even if he is sincere in heart and a genius. Remember that! The people will meet the atheist and overcome him, and Russia will be one and orthodox.' Do you really believe that is about to happen, Anatoly Mironovitch?"

The officer is taken a little aback. "Well, admittedly, so far, there is only silence," he concedes quietly.

The other Russian, a nimble, self-educated peasant, quickly comes to his rescue. "Yes—silence, but what kind of silence?" he challenges shrewdly. "This silence is important, but it is not well understood by most of us Russians." He pauses, pondering how to proceed. "Look, I've seen this sort of thing in my own village. The atheistic village council wanted to set up—what do you call it, for a radio—?"

"Loudspeaker," I prompt.

"An antenna?" the officer guesses.

"That's it, an antenna," the peasant seizes the strange word gratefully. "The antenna is to be erected on top of the church. When the villagers spot the local commissar and several armed Red Guards at the church, they all hurry over. Suddenly it's a mob scene. The whole village has gathered in front of the church. For a minute or two they watch in silence.

"Then an old peasant speaks up. 'Comrad Commissar, you can't do that.' 'Can't do what? Who decides what can or can't be done around here, eh?'

"The crowd is turning ugly. There is a lot of muttering and scolding—even some open threats.

"A husky young peasant, shouldering an axe, steps forward. 'Comrades. We won't allow you to put that devil's machine up on the church.'

"The commissar calmly ignores the threat. At his command a ladder is placed against the church steeple. Two more peasants, armed with pitch forks, join the young man in front of the ladder. The first young man has had enough. 'All right,' he bellows, 'If you want to get your skulls split open—come on! Now beat it, beat it!'

"The commissar looks around at his guards who, although armed, don't look as if they relish the confrontation. Hastily the commissar confers with his men. Then, in sullen silence, they pack up their—what's it called again?—pick up the ladder and take off. And they don't come back either."

"That's Russian activism for you," Father Nikolai says proudly.

"It's a defensive war," says the old officer reflectively.

"The peasant's lot has always forced him into that role," Wolff adds.

These optimistic discussions and anecdotes have the effect of raising our flagging spirits somewhat.

"This is the end," Wolff whispers to me one evening when he comes in. He is pale and shaken. *"Gospodi pomilui!"*

"What's happened?"

"You can't imagine, Sasha. Down there below the cutting area"—he points southward—"near where they found Neufeld, dozens of bodies lying in the swamp—men, women, children. We saw them just now. It's horrible—black, dried up faces, mouths full of clay, arms and legs sprawled every which way—twenty, thirty—God knows how many.

"Suicides?"

"Who gives a damn? That's a mere technicality."

He sits down and puffs out his cheeks in horror. "Sasha—this is the end, I tell you. To be deprived—that's one thing. Sickness, hunger . . . all bad enough. But to croak like that. No, no I can't take it."

He frightens me. I've never seen Wolff so completely unnerved. "Are they German or Russian, or what—?"

"Filthy, stinking ragdolls—dead ragdolls! That's what they are. What race is that? O my God!"

For the rest of the evening Wolff is silent and withdrawn. Koehn and the others continue to talk obsessively about the tragic scene. Apparently the work gang had been taken home by a different route tonight to oblige one of the guards, who had a message to deliver in one of the other barracks. And that is how they came to see the grisly sight.

I foresee a bad night for Wolff; and it comes, but a few nights later than I had anticipated.

Three more days pass. It's a very cold night. Even the mosquitoes spare us for once. The men are snoring. Here and there a child scratches and whimpers in pain. Then silence again.

For some reason I can't fall asleep. I look across at Wolff. He is very restless and tosses about in his bunk muttering broken words and phrases. Is he asleep or awake?

"Wolff?"

"Yeah, right away," he slurs thickly. He must think it's morning. He starts up slowly, pulls his blanket around his shoulders and sits upright on his bunk. He is shivering violently and there is a strange look on his face—the rigid expression of a sleepwalker.

" 'And I saw,' " he begins to recite in a weird monotone, " '. . . behold a white horse . . . he that sat on him had a bow; and . . . crown was given . . . him; and he went . . . conquering . . . .' "

I squeeze my eyes shut. I feel sick as I listen to that harsh, lifeless voice, so different froom Wolff's usually animated tone.

He continues to recite with frightening accuracy. Does he know the whole of Revelations from memory?

" '. . . and lo . . . black horse and . . . had balances in his hand . . . A measure of wheat for a penny . . .' Ha-ha . . . 'and hurt not . . . oil and wine'—ha-ha-ha-haaaaa—oil and wine . . . ."

Wolff begins to rock from the waist. His whole body is shaking under his blanket. He is quiet for a few moments. A night bird oboes in the forest. A chorus of sighs rises from the trees all around. Then he starts again. The whole thing is getting to be eerie. Should I call out? Wake him?

" '. . . sat on him was Death . . . Hell followed . . . And power was given . . . to kill . . . with sword and . . . hunger'—heh, Comrade Commissar, as far as hunger."

He slides off his bunk and stands up swaying. His voice comes in gasping sobs now. " '. . . sacred . . . Lord . . . how long willt . . . judge and not . . . avenge . . . our blood . . . against those . . . dwell on . . . earth . . . .?' "

A long sigh, then silence. For a moment he stands staring unseeingly at the dark wall. Then he lies down, huddled and sobbing under his blanket.

Didn't any of the others hear him? I get up and feel Wolff's brow. It is dry and burning. So Wolff has finally been stricken too, the last of our group to get sick.

The night frosts are back again. I try to keep Wolff warm by piling all his and my extra clothes on top of his blanket. His fever hangs on for days and he is delirious much of the time. At least he doesn't recite Revelations again. He has been stricken from the work list, but he is not deemed sick enough to be taken to the hospital, which is overflowing with victims of hunger-typhus. The dread disease has struck the back section of our barrack. In one day seven people are taken away. Since Andreievka can't take any more patients, these latest victims are taken over rough roads to Ustjug, sixty-five kilometers away. Wolff seems to be suffering from nothing worse than a relatively mild form of malaria.

"They'll be buried enroute, anyway," Koehn says gloomily. We have become pretty callous about such things.

I decide to try working again. It will be hard, but I'm starving on barracks ration. My gift package was used up long ago.

After taking her children to the nursery, Anna Zimmermann disappears for the whole day. Around eleven at night she returns with a parcel.

"Some flour for the children," she confides to Koehn. She now avoids me. "I searched all over. It's getting to be almost impossible to find. The famine has struck the hunting villages too. Zyrians, Russians—it's the same all over."

She pours her flour into a pail and sits down. She looks flustered and worn-out.

"How did you manage to get it? What's the price of flour now?" Koehn inquires with an odd expression on his face.

Mrs. Zimmermann is silent for a moment. "Expensive—a head of female hair for five kilograms."

She takes off her babushka; her long auburn tresses are gone. What remains of her hair clings to her head like a ragged skull cap.

I give her a long look and wonder who would be generous enough to give her five kilograms of flour for her hair.

The rumor about the releases is confirmed at last. Ohm Peters and his grandson, the Albrecht lad, are to return home. Koehn agonizes for a long time before deciding to send his children back.

"Perhaps things will be a little easier for them down there," he rationalizes; "they miss their mother's care here."

Mrs. Zimmermann would like to send her two younger children south, but has nowhere to send them. She complains bitterly about her bad luck.

Ohm Peters comes shuffling over to my bunk. He's finding it difficult to leave.

"Alexander, I wanted to stay with you all; you need someone here who can give you a word of consolation when you need it. But it's getting to be beyond my strength. I'm seventy-three, but I'll try to find a roof and some food for the children. Perhaps—," he stops, embarrassed.

I feel sorry for him. He knows he must appear almost selfish to us now.

I try to reassure him. "Ohm Jasch, I'm—we're all—very happy for you. You have meant even more to us here than you did in the good times back home. All of us are forever indebted to you. Give our greetings at home—if that is still what it is," I add absently. I see I'm making his departure more difficult for him. "I mean home—Mariental," I finish lamely.

"Yes, yes," he agrees, "you're right. Since we have lost God here in Russia, we've also lost the true meaning of home. And so everything has come unraveled."

He's incredible, this lovable old man. Every misfortune takes on some spiritual significance for him.

Ohm Peters reaches into his pocket. "Alexander, we've gone beyond pious talk in this place. We need more than bread here. Only God can be our staff of life in this horrid camp. Here, my personal bequest. For you—and Volodya Wolff, when he's well enough to read."

He offers me his battered little Bible with a gentle smile. "You saw how it was torn apart once, but it's still a living whole, as God is a living whole."

He shakes hands with all of us before he is taken to the Command Post with the children.

The empty bunks don't remain empty for long. This time a broad-shouldered, elderly Mennonite and his family from Ufa are sent to us. The wife is tiny and delicate and has a crooked back. They have six children, of whom the eldest is a husky lad of about sixteen. The man is friendly but reserved, a trait that is typical of our colonists.

The children, especially the younger ones, are in a pitiful state. Their withered bodies are clothed in crude smocks which their mother has fashioned from sacks. For footwear they have dirty foot-cloths and ragged bast shoes.

Somebody mentions the name Schmidt. Koehn slaps his brow. "Schmidt of Ufa? Of course! Do you know who he is? He's the entrepreneur who owned at least half a dozen steam mills in Ufa and vicinity. Dear God—! It's a wonder he's still alive. I thought men of his kind had all been done away with long ago."

Wolff is on the mend again. His fever is gone and he is beginning to talk, although his voice sounds weak and hollow. In the evening, I sit beside his bunk, pleased to see him taking an interest in things again.

"I'm glad you've decided to stick around, Volodya. We need you here," I tell him the first evening he is feeling better.

His strangely altered eyes hold mine and he does not smile. "That was only the second act, Sasha. The final curtain is still to come. You know, these real-life tragedies are different from Shakespeare's, where the fools provide comic relief after the sad scenes. In our little drama there are no funny scenes—only sadder ones."

"Yeah, but you mustn't make it sound as though you're writing this tragedy by yourself."

"You're right, my friend . . .. What's been happening?"

"Nothing much, except that Ohm Peters and the kids left for home while you were wrestling with your fever."

"In spite of everything! Lucky man. Sasha, I'd like to make one more visit down there—just to see everything again—and then I'd be ready to . . . depart. But, of course, I know I won't."

I fuss around his bed without answering. I don't want him to notice that I share his premonition.

One evening the eldest Schmidt boy comes into the barrack lugging a full sack on his back. I watch as he lowers it to the floor. The soft contents spread the sack.

"Flour?"

"Meat!"

"Meat?"

He opens the sack. "Horsemeat!" he chuckles. I'm convinced by the horrible stench. The magenta-colored chunks are mottled with green.

"Where did you get it?"

"Out there, from the clearing—by the ash trees."

Now I know. "From the cadaver?"

"So what? It's meat, isn't it? Cook it and it's good!" he says firmly. "In Vyatka we ate hampsters and rats; horsemeat is better."

The carrion spreads its foul odor through the barrack, but the Schmidt children appear not to be bothered by it. They peer into the sack eagerly and the little girl of eight claps her hands ecstatically.

After many months I receive a letter from home. Actually, I'd rather not hear from them anymore. It's too painful.

"And your parents and brother and sister?" Koehn inquires, as an old friend of the family.

"Heinrich has escaped—China! But the others—" I begin to read the letter. Every sentence is painful: "From our village ten are in prison because they threshed a little grain for themselves on the sly. The prison in Saratov is overflowing, they say. All are classified as 'saboteurs against collectivization.' Most people in the colony are subsisting on turnips and dogmeat." There is more of the same kind of news.

"Are you by chance still interested in such gay tunes?" I hold out the letter to Wolff.

He waves it off. "This is more interesting, Sasha." He is reading *Pravda*. " 'French President Herriot tours Soviet Russia.' There's a picture for you!"

The picture shows Herriot standing in shirtsleeves as the guest of honor of a *kolkhoz*. With a broad politician's smile he is handing a pail of something to a suitably awed-looking worker.

"Just look at that shirt: white and embroidered in silk. A gold watch chain suspended across his big stomach. The man is laughing. What is Herriot laughing at?"

Wolff looks at us amused. The cheerful cynic in him is not quite dead after all. "And to think there are people who have doubts about Soviet Russia. My darling Russia, Mecca for European tourists."

"Where did you get the paper?"

"Erwin Zimmermann brought it home from the nursery school. At least our children are learning about socialist optimism earlier than we did."

Our letters to Germany have virtually ceased now that three people from our camp have been sent to Solovki for sending "counter-revolutionary reports" abroad.

What has not ceased is our gallows humor, which is getting more and more macabre. "After Solovki, you won't see me," somebody rhymes.

"Better to keep mum in camp, and bear the hunger cramp," somebody else adds.

"Listen to this ghoulish academy of poets," Wolff says contemptuously. "Are we all becoming unfeeling brutes?"

"Perhaps our hunger pangs are the only feelings we have left, Volodya?" Wolff shakes his head bitterly.

In Schmidt's section, as Koehn calls it, two of the girls wake up one night in a panic.

"I can't see . . . it's so dark," one of them wails in confusion. The other girl is howling even louder.

Wolff is awake. "The electrification of Russia is high on the list of socialist priorities," he quotes in a whisper.

Mrs. Schmidt has trouble finding a match. Finally it flares in the darkness. A tiny candle gives a flickering little light. Somebody stumbles. This is followed by scoldings. There are more cries.

"Shhh—! you've got a light!"

"But I can't see anything at all," one of the girls bawls in terror.

The mother, thoroughly alarmed, moans and soothes simultaneously.

I think I know what's wrong. I get up and walk over. "Don't worry, Mrs. Schmidt," I whisper, "this sort of thing is common here. It's a temporary blindness caused by malnutrition. In Number Eight four children had these attacks, but after two or three weeks their vision was back to normal again."

The afflicted children gradually calm down and go back to sleep. What I haven't told Mrs. Schmidt is that not all the children recover their vision completely. Some are left with permanently impaired eyesight.

Old man Schmidt has been missing for several days. Now Comma is making inquiries, but nobody knows anything. Has he perished in the forest? Run away? No, he wouldn't just abandon his family; none of us believes that. Because the older children are suffering from malaria and can't go to work, Schmidt's family has been without bread since his disappearance. And the two younger children are still suffering from hunger-blindness. The family is in desperate straits.

We make inquiries everywhere, but nobody can tell us anything.

On the fourth day, just before dark, Schmidt returns. He is carrying a large bundle on his back. He is utterly exhausted. Sweat is pouring down his face and his eyes are glazed with fatigue.

The children hardly notice him. Their concern is with the bundle he lets fall to the floor. With a deep groan, he collapses in a heap beside the pack. Mrs. Schmidt does her best to rouse him, but he seems to be in a deep coma. A trickle of blood appears at the corner of his mouth as he lies huddled on the floor.

I feel his pulse. It is very weak. Mrs. Schmidt kneels beside her husband, sobbing. The children also become alarmed for their father. Now the blood is streaming into his beard. He is hemorrhaging internally. But from what? Is it a heart attack or has he been wounded somewhere? I examine him as best I can but find no wounds or marks. It must be something internal.

We move the stricken man to his bunk and keep trying to revive him. But he does not open his eyes again.

"Just to get some lousy bread—goddamnit anyway!" grates a voice in the background.

A few days after Schmidt's tragic death we are dealt an even more personal blow. Father Nikolai and the silent Tatar are working on a large pine tree near Koehn and me. They are having trouble sawing through the thick trunk. The saw keeps sticking in the cut as the tree begins to list slightly. Father Nikolai kneels in the snow trying to work loose the saw blade and the Tatar reaches for his axe to chop around the blade to free it. He chops twice, viciously; on the third stroke the axe head flies off and strikes Father Nikolai squarely on the forehead.

The priest lies crumpled in the snow bleeding; his eyes and mouth are open. He is still breathing, but his condition is critical. The Tatar is in a state of shock. He prostrates himself beside the unconscious victim and cries over and over:

"It was an accident, Little Father, an accident. Allah allowed the axe head to fly off, Little Father. Forgive me, Little Father—forgive me."

To distract the Tatar we ask him to help us lash together a crude litter. He obeys, still dazed and muttering apologies.

Miraculously, the priest is still alive when we get him to the barrack. With heavy hearts we place him on his bunk. He has not recovered consciousness.

We are in a terrible quandary. Should we try to rush the injured man to the hospital, or do we just wait for him to die? After cleaning the wound, Koehn turns to me: "It's hopeless, Sasha. I don't see how he can still be breathing. He'd never last to Andreievka."

We begin our death vigil. At one point Father Nikolai's lips begin to stir, as though he is struggling for speech. But no sound comes and soon the lips stop moving. I take his pulse again. It is very weak now.

By morning the priest is gone. We decide to notify his Russian friends in Camp 509. While waiting for them, Wolff and I go through Father Nikolai's meagre personal effects. Except for the vestments and instruments of his priestly office, there is almost nothing of a personal nature in his belongings. We find only a few letters from a sister in Samara and some from a fellow priest in Tashkent. There is also the New Testament he received from Ohm Peters. We can find no other signs of a private life.

"It's as though he had no personal identity apart from the Church," Wolff says with admiring gravity. "He was a saint, Sasha, and saints aren't individuals in the same sense as the rest of us. Their lives are open books in public, closed books in private. The mystery that surrounds their personalities is God's mystery. It's the mystery of self-sacrificing love. It's a love that demands nothing for itself, and so does not feed the kind of ego we identify as individual personality. Ohm Peters also had this disdain for personal identity. Do you remember how he gave away every personal possession in his chest the Christmas before last?"

"Perhaps, Volodya, men like Father Nikolai and Ohm Peters have private identities we are simply unaware of because they are too deep and inaccessible to ordinary mortals like us."

"You may be right, Sasha. In any case, he was a man of God and we were lucky to have him with us here." He pauses and looks reflective. "By the way, did you ever wonder why he stayed here in our barrack even after he had found his Russian 'congregation' in another camp. Strange isn't it?"

"Yes, I've thought about that too, Volodya, and I can't explain it. Perhaps he felt bound to us simply through the experiences we had shared since being thrown together."

"Perhaps. Or could it be that by staying with us rather than with his own people he was laying some kind of private penance on himself?"

As a remembrance of Father Nikolai we decide to keep the little New Testament book he prized so much.

Time no longer seems to matter much to any of us. We survive, but we feel neither hope nor despair. On a gentle day in August we go for a long walk and sit in the sun on the edge of the forest. Nearby lies Yenisseievka.

Koehn has a pensive, faraway look. "Do you realize, friends, that we three are the last ones?"

Wolff, looking very tried, is listlessly watching a woodpecker and pretends not to hear.

"Yeah, our original group now consists of three dying men and a couple of doomed widows," Koehn adds sombrely.

Again, neither Wolff nor I feel like picking up Koehn's remark.

The late summer sun peers uncertainly among the grey and brown trunks. The leaves are already turning color. The brief northern summer is waning and another winter is about to descend. Only the pines stand green and solid, unchanged from the day of our arrival. Nearby are the fields where we used to spend our rest days. Weeds are growing among the dry, sparse stubble. The feeble crop has long since been harvested.

As the wind gusts colder, we pull our rags more tightly around our skinny bodies and gaze out into the distance where to the south the pine forest stretches like a long, dark fortification.

Wolff suddenly stops humming. He gets up and takes a few stiff steps forward. He is like a man in a trance.

"In case somebody should ever . . . after us," he mutters and points to the west, his dark eyes still searching beyond the trees. "God in his mercy grant that our world beyond the frozen Mezen be remembered as a real world with ordinary, decent, suffering, and praying people in it. Let them know there *was* a Camp Number 513 here, and a Barrack Number seven containing people who lived and loved and hoped in the midst of despair—as long as they could.

"It was all so senseless. Many of us fell from despair to apathy to nothing. But there were those—Waldemar Wolff of Saratov for one, and Peter Koehn of Mariental for another, and Alexander Harms for a third—who in spite of bitter afflictions, in the end found in the brutal forests of Archangel peace and resignation. And whoever hears about us should know that we did not forget to bless the—"

Epilogue

Peace and resignation! Wolff is right, of course. If our suffering here has any meaning at all it is that we have gone beyond hatred and love to a spiritual condition that surpasses all understanding. In spite of everything we are at peace here amidst God's immortal, unspeaking green sentinels of the taiga. What did Wolff say just now? That we did not forget to bless the—what? Yes, yes, that we did not forget to bless the people, the uncounted millions, who were *not* here, who knew nothing about the unspeakable misery and degradation and pain and hopelessness we have endured here. We have won the power—no! we have earned the right to bless and forgive not only those who put us here, but also those who do not even know of our existence. Through our suffering we have won the freedom to bless!

I see again Tielmann standing tall and solemn in the swaying boxcar as he recites Ehrenburg's *Prayer for Russia.* How did the lines go? "For our unloving hearts . . . For those who cannot pray . . . For those wielding knives and spears, And for those who howl like dogs, Let us pray in peace to God."

And what was it that Wolff said to his Martha that day in the forest when he was trying to comfort her about Theresa's defection? Yes—that the real subject of our studies in this harsh school could be summed up in one word—"nothing." He was right, but what he didn't see then was that in the condition of "nothing" we would find everything, that for us true spiritual liberty could come only after we had become nothing.

I see now that Ohm Peters and Father Nikolai were always free here because in their own minds and hearts they had become nothing long before.

For nothingness triumphant, let us pray in peace to God.